MY SECOND CHANCE WITH HER

AJIT KUMAR

INDIA · SINGAPORE · MALAYSIA

ISBN 979-8-89133-886-9

CONTENTS

Chapter 1

THE OFFICE

Saabji... Phone side me rakh ke cross kijiye. The security guard told me to keep the phone in the wooden box kept on the table before I passed through the 'walk-through metal detector.'

Things are so different in these multinational companies. Back in college, we thought that offices would be a place of substance, a place where we would be respected, a place where we would be pestered by salutes all the time, and there would be guards who would stand up on seeing us. We would be addressed as 'sir' all the time. God, wasn't I wrong? Leave alone the salutes; these guys would literally shout at you the moment they saw something wrong in you or, to put it more precisely, something wrong 'ON' you.

But again, these guys were just doing what they were paid to do. I had no reason to take this personally; I did what he told me to do and entered the office.

Every day I came here hoping to get used to it, with the same belief I went there each day. Unfortunately, that day never came... I'm still trying to get used to it... maybe someday I'll find it in me to start liking it, but today wasn't that day. Believe me, this was an extremely depressing place, not a single moment went by when I didn't regret busting my ass off in college so that I could land one of "these."

As I entered the office, one of the most beautiful voices fell on my ears: "Good morning, Ajeete."

It was Anjali; she greeted me every morning with the sweetest possible smile. When the smile reached her eyes, it twinkled. She did this with her head tilted sideways ever so slightly that made her look like a little pretty doll, and the way she extended the "good" was the real icing on the cake. The wonderful part was that she did it every day, day in and day out.

I courteously smiled back at her. To be honest, she was one of the reasons I came to the office. In fact, the high point of my day was when I saw her. But as is the case in most love stories, for her, I was just a "good friend." She considered us to be such good friends that she even took the liberty of tweaking my name; I do not remember when Ajit became Ajeete. Actually, I did not mind this little tweak; the personal touch in it appealed to me.

She looked particularly beautiful today in her purple top. One of the best things about her was her hair; they were surprisingly bouncy with a slight curl at the tips. This, along with her plump cheeks, made her look really cute. Was it her plump cheeks or her bubbly demeanor? I don't know, but I always had a strong urge to call her 'Gappu,' but I was always overtly conscious about how she would react if I ever did that.

After exchanging pleasantries, I started my system and began reading the morning news online. This was how I started my day - to get to know what is going on in the world before I got sucked into my own little world of codes and bugs.

I was busy going through the paper when Anjali rolled her chair towards mine and said, "Did you hear Sanjay resigned? He is not even waiting to serve his notice period."

I did not know who this Sanjay guy was, but I was happy for him. At least he was escaping this hell. "Sahi hai, good for him. So is there a party?" I asked.

"Ha hai na cafeteria me... chal chalte hai... let's go," she said.

We stood up and headed towards the cafeteria. On reaching there, we saw a huge commotion; people were hustling around, running back and forth between the cafeteria and the celebration table. Since I was having difficulty placing this Sanjay, I didn't picture him to be a popular figure, but looking at the surroundings, I stood corrected.

Finally, all was in order, and he started cutting the cake. Everyone had something to say about him, something nice. This is one of the many good things you get to experience when you've resigned. People speak good things about you, how you were a great team player, how your colleagues learned things from you, and the icing on the cake comes when your manager tells what an asset you'd been to the team. The same manager who never passed up an opportunity to demean you could actually be seen praising you. Hearing some of those things might get you thinking, 'Wow, I really am a good man.'

Sanjay's last day reminded me of one such last day, which I had experienced, the last day of my college.

The memory of leaving college is still fresh in my mind, how we were bidding each other adieu with tears filling our eyes. Watching guys cry is one thing, but watching an engineer cry is a totally different thing. There were eyes that had not dropped a single tear even during the toughest phase of ragging; there were eyes that had seen all the possible adversities in life over the past 4 years, yet not a drop rolled down those cheeks. But that day was something special - not a single eye was there that was not moist. No one was being beaten up, no one was being bullied, no results were declared, no girl had turned down any proposal. Yet there was relentless crying, no words came, just tears flowed.

Recollecting those moments, I felt a lump in my throat, I felt heavy in my heart. Something was amiss, don't know what, but something didn't feel right. I could have paid anything to be in college again. I was recollecting the glorious past when I heard a shrill South Indian tone.

"Yajit (Ajit)... Where are you, sir? Have some cake," Sanjay was holding a big piece in his hand, and it seemed as if he was threatening to smear it on my face. I smiled politely and ate the piece. Before concluding the party, his line manager gave a small speech, thanking him for his contribution to the project and the company as a whole.

People started walking back to their workstations, each with a different emotion on their face. Some were happy for getting the morning cake, while others were saddened by their friend leaving. I gingerly returned to my station and unlocked my system; it was time for work. The morning party had already taken up my newspaper time, so I opened my mailbox. There was an email from our client office at the offshore division. These emails never came with good news. Fearing the worst, I double-clicked the link, and as I had suspected, it was no good news. It read:

A major bug reported in your code, the report tracking the daily expenditure of the customer that was supposed to be printed fails when there are multiple customers with the same name. This should have been the basic test criteria. This sort of unprofessionalism is simply unacceptable.

I had barely finished reading the email when I saw my line manager coming out of his chamber; apparently, he too had been cc'ed. I did not expect him to come so fast. I was still figuring out what could have gone wrong, and now the manager was coming, probably demanding an explanation. He came directly towards my desk and took the mouse; he was furious. I did not know how to react; I quietly slid out from my chair and stood up.

"Do you care to explain, Mr. Ajit?" He asked point-blank.

Actually, I did not have anything to explain. I mean, how could anyone explain this?

It was a slip-up on my end, and I should deal with it. I was prepared to face the music; it was my fault. But just as I was about to admit my mistake, a stroke of brilliance struck me, or at least I thought it was brilliant. I just replied curtly:

"Sir... Yes, I admit that it was a slip-up on my part, but I don't think I should be blamed for this."

"What are you trying to imply?" He asked. I could see his face turn red. I should have taken this sign and stopped, but I didn't. In fact, I started to defend myself vociferously, and in the heat of the moment, I replied:

"I mean that there is a review team and a testing team in place; they are supposed to catch bugs of these types before we release it to our clients. I am not saying that I am not at fault, but I cannot take the entire blame for this. Technically, once the code is through our testing cycle, I should not be held responsible for any issue that crops up later."

I spilled out everything in a single breath. I did not know how I gathered the courage to do this, but I just let myself loose at him. And if I thought that this would not have repercussions, I was wrong, I was wrong big time, because in the corporate world, it's things like these that have repercussions, and I had just invited one for myself. This just set off the bomb that every manager carries inside themselves; the bomb that needs just one trigger and 'boom!!!!!!' it goes off. I could not even begin to describe how the next 10 – 12 minutes went for me.

He was yelling at the top of his voice. Initially, it was related to my work and the screw-up that had happened, and then things deviated. Here I must say there are three stages in a 'yelling' match that a manager throws at you:

It starts with the original screw-up, the thing that was originally responsible for the entire debacle.

Once this phase is over, up comes the past screw-ups, mostly those are not relevant, but since he is the manager and he has to scold you, the past needs to be dug up, as without this, the entire match would be over within the first few minutes.

If you've not had many significant screw-ups in the past, be ready to find out the flaws in your attitude. In my case, my "lack of attitude" somehow got traced back to my college.

"I don't remember how, but it seemed that my college was responsible for my supposed 'attitude problem'."

I had to endure the entire three phases, and why? Because I had a 'stroke of brilliance!!!'.

However, I never expected it to go as badly as this. People were peeping from their workstations. It was kind of an amusing thing for them. It was not a good day for me, but for these folks, it was one of the most entertaining days - first the farewell party and then this screaming party... they ought to be loving it.

Finally, the session ended, and there was some kind of normalcy restored. After he was satisfied that I had been humiliated enough, he went back to his chamber, and his exact departing words were 'Look out, Ajit, you're on thin ice'.

I did not pay heed to what he said. These kinds of things between managers and engineers happen on a regular basis, and there was nothing to read between the lines on this issue.

After the manager left, I almost involuntarily took my phone out and started typing a message on it: 'Maar liya be aaj boss ne... Worst possible start to the day... Tum log sunao' and sent it to my messaging group PZ.

PZ was a messaging group that the guys from my hostel had formed to stay in touch after the days in college was over, and the group was named after our hostel, PentaZeppelin.

How PZ started is an interesting story in itself:

I distinctly remember the day it happened. It had been 2 months since I left college. I was still coming to terms with the new life that had been forced on me. Did I have an option, or for that matter does anyone have, can anyone fight the invincible (time)? While in college, fun and frolic had become a part of our lives. The interesting part about all those things was that we did not realize how wonderful it was until it got snatched off, and suddenly we were in a 'JOB'. All those mass bunk, missing classes for petty reasons, it was all gone, and there was nothing left.

I was lost in these thoughts of yesteryears when my mobile beeped; it was a message from 'Yashasvi Pal'. I thought it was another regular message from 'Paliya' as we used to call him fondly. I read it but really couldn't understand. It probably wasn't for me; it might have been one of those mistakes that happen, an honest mistake.

What I did not realize back then was that it was the beginning of a new era. That message actually triggered an avalanche. There were messages flowing from all corners of India, 'Gautam Kumar Das' aka 'GKD' from Kolkata, 'Paliya', 'Mishra', 'Rashid' from Delhi, Bibhakar aka 'Gahori (Assamese for PIG)' from Mangalore (Down South), Ranawat 'Rinku' from Gujarat, to name a few.

In short, we had the entire nation covered. Thus came into existence the SMS chat group 'PZ Live'.

Many would find it hard to believe, but we guys from PZ (PentaZeppelin) are still in touch with each other, and not just in a customary manner.

Games are still played, maybe not on LAN anymore, but on a common server through the internet. Guys are not woken up in the morning by kicks and bangs on the door, but by a series of messages and missed calls. All in all, this messaging group was a masterstroke that had helped us to stay in touch with each other.

We shared all the details, our daily ups and downs with the guys, and it helped, it sure did. The fact that I knew there was a system in place where I could vent off my feelings gave me the strength to endure the cruelty of corporate life. It gave me an assurance that there are shoulders out there on which I could cry on, there are ears out there that are willing to hear me when I need to say something, there are brains out there busy finding ways to bail me out of any trouble that I could get into.

I was staring at my phone thinking about the past and smiling wryly when someone patted me on my shoulder.

I looked around; it was Nisha. She must have heard about the bashing I had got.

"It's OK Ajit... Managers aise hi hote hai, don't be upset."

She was my immediate lead, and to me, she was like an elder sister. She was from Kerala but brought up in Mumbai.

She had a distinct nasal dominance in her accent, which suggested that she still she had a bit of Kerala left in her.

"Oh no... It's not that. Theek hai, there was something wrong in the code, and someone had to be held responsible for that, nothing personal." I tried to downplay the issue. I knew the workings of IT industry inside out, and the only thing that annoyed me was being made the scapegoat.

“Sahi hai phir.... It's all good then. Shall we go for breakfast? Bahut bhook lagi hai,” Nisha asked.

It was customary for us to have breakfast together before starting the day's work; Anjali, Nisha, and I had breakfast together every day.

"Sure, but I... Sorry, we just had a big piece of cake." I said with a big sarcastic smile. “Arre re... Mere liye nahi rakha,” Nisha said in a complaining tone.

She had this singular style of talking; the way she used the words ‘Arre re,’ ‘haa re bol,’ ‘theek hai na,’ etc., seemed like her signature.

“Itna hi khane ka mann tha to pehle kyu nahi aayi, you should have come earlier,” Anjali jumped in.

Nisha was Anjali's lead too, but they had this rapport which surpassed the boundaries of the official hierarchy. She just smiled in response to her comment, and we headed towards the cafeteria, for the second time today.

“Haa re bol... what was the issue?” Nisha asked. To be honest, I had placed a bet against myself on how long it would be before she asked this.

"Actually, the code that I'd been working on last week..."

"Which one... the report generator?" she asked before I could complete.

"Ya... there was a problem in it, I had not validated the case in which there are multiple customers with the same name," I explained to her.

"Ha... theek hai na, but this should have been there in the requirements, as a developer, we should just stick to what is there in the sheet, right?" Anjali added, and she was correct. They had not mentioned this in their requirement sheet, but again, what was supposed to happen had happened, and there was no point in crying over spilled milk.

"Yes, it was not there in the requirement sheet that was given to me, so being a developer, I developed what I was told to do, and then it went to the code review team. If something was amiss, they should have pointed it out there. These issues should ideally have been reported by the testing team. Now, if they missed it, I shouldn't be held responsible solely," I said.

"Haa to sahi kiya... You should not have stood there silently and taken the blame on yourself," Anjali supported me.

"Arre nahi re... After all, he is our manager; uspe bhi bahut questions raise hote hai, I don't think it was personal," Nisha said, sounding as if she was trying to defend him. Being a lead herself, I could imagine the sympathy.

"Ha, theek hai, he said what he was supposed to say, and I said what I felt like saying, so all's good," I was trying my best to play down the issue as much as I could.

They got the hint and dropped the topic; we finished our meal and headed back towards our workstations.

My manager was standing next to my station; he put his hands on his hips, widened his eyes, and furrowed his eyebrows upon seeing me. The look was enough to say, "You're screwed." I gathered all the courage that I could and went towards him.

"This is exactly what I was talking about; you screw up something and then instead of fixing it right away, you go off to the cafeteria. You had just come from Suresh's party, right? How did you get so hungry suddenly... tell me..." he yelled at the top of his lungs.

"I'll do it right away," I replied in a sedate tone.

I was at fault here, and I was guarding myself from having another "stroke of brilliance." This was by far the worst day I've ever had, and it seemed like it had just started. I quietly slid into my chair and started working on the issue. Like I said, this was not the best day that I was having, and I was not going to risk anything. I knew any delay, and he would've exploded for sure. The issue that had been reported wasn't a big one; all that was needed was another validation to check whether there were customers with the same names, and then change the identification criteria. I did it, and within 20 minutes, the code was up and running. I went over to the manager's chamber and informed him about the completion of the job.

"Good... make sure this doesn't happen again in future."

This wasn't the response I was expecting; this made me revisit the entire "not personal" theory. Had it not been personal, he would definitely have appreciated my efforts. But again, there was nothing I could have done; I mean there is no way you can force appreciation out of someone. So I walked out silently, and everybody kept their dignity.

Things are expected to go haywire when you are working for any organization, but the way it panned out today made me feel really bad. On most other days I was the best performer, even though I did not like being here. Still, I always put in my 100%. But today things were different; from being "that," I became the guy who was bashed by the manager. It may not have been a big deal for others, but I wasn't able to digest this. I became really angry, angry at my manager's behavior, angry at the code reviewer who overlooked the problem in the code, and angry at the client who shot that mail when he had clearly overlooked this requirement.

I learned one thing about anger that day: the more you hold it inside, the more it compounds.

I sat at my desk, hoping that a few quiet moments would help me relax, but I couldn't stop thinking about it, and the more I thought, the angrier I got. In a fit of rage, I banged the desk.

"Ajit... kya hua? What happened?" Anjali came and asked. I was so angry at that moment that had it been any other person there, I would have given them a piece of my mind, but it was Anjali, and I, in good sense, couldn't spill my anger on her.

"Did he say something bad?" she asked.

"No... But why should I be held responsible for this? I did whatever I was told to do. Now when the defect was found, I rectified it, and still, this is what I get." I voiced my disappointment.

"This is how it works, Ajeet. Maybe he is having an off day today. Pick yourself up, dust yourself off, and start working. Forget about everything and just focus on the job at hand." She wasn't even aware of what happened in there; she was just being philosophical.

"Anjali, you know this better than anyone else. What you are saying is easier said than done. But yes, there is no point being hung over this issue. Magar kya kare, gussa hai aa jaata hai."

I hoped she would stop talking, as I was getting irritated by the minute, and I was afraid if I reached my breaking point, I wouldn't be able to control myself and end up doing or saying something that I would regret.

"Chal, theek hai... I hope you hold yourself together," she said and went back to her station.

I went back to my daily work and tried to get the disappointment off my head, but it kept coming back intermittently to haunt me. I was just looking forward to the end of the day now. After the disappointing day that it was, I went back to my room. The traffic en route to my home was getting on my nerves. The stretch between my office in Vikhroli and my flat in Bhandup wasn't more than 4 km, and it took nearly half an hour for me to commute. This had not bothered me earlier, but today it did, it was getting on my nerves. I was already irritable, and this wasn't helping my mood.

Finally, after battling the noisy traffic, I reached my home. The same place which I called "ROOM" before suddenly became "HOME" today. Somehow, I felt a sense of assurance here. There was no one around, and this was a good thing because it meant that there would be no one to pick on me. I kicked off my shoes, went directly to my bed, and lay there. I didn't even bother to turn on the lights. I reached out for my pack of cigarettes, lit one, and started puffing away on it. I began thinking about how life had changed after college. In college, the "FINAL FRONTIER" for a student was to get a job, who would have thought this is what it would turn out to be. I started recalling how I got my job, all those events that transpired leading to it. I was on the verge of breaking down after getting rejected by companies left and right, and one such rejection nearly pushed me over the line.

Chapter 2

HOSTEL

"You don't understand my situation; you have no idea what I am experiencing, so just fuck off!!!!" I blurted out at Yadav.

'Poor man, he had just come to console me, console me for getting rejected all over again. Was the word "Loser" written large over my face? Why the hell do I get rejected all the time? And now I spilled the fluids of my frustration on him.

"Arre koi baat nahi, it happens they don't see the things in you, someone will, so just cheer up, asshole." These words weren't enough. I didn't speak fearing that I may end up squirting pleasantries on him again. What I had forgotten is that it takes quite a lot to piss him off.

I wondered how life in college was incomplete without these pleasantries.

Anyway, this sulking wouldn't have helped me. I needed to devise a plan, a plan that would help me get through this horrible phase. I needed to plan and plan real quick. Time was running out of hand, and when it came to planning stuff, no one came close to the might of Shantanu Paul, such a plotter he was. I recall an incident of our first semester in college;

Everyone was busy preparing for the chemistry lab exams, memorizing the tests to determine the salt contents. However, that genius mind had something else in store. In the exams, we were given a pouch with some number written on it, and to make things difficult, the pouches had salt colored in the same color so that we could not guess its content. This got Shantanu thinking, "if all the pouches are colored, how the hell will the dumb-headed teachers remember its content? There has to be something in the code; we have to crack it, guys, we have to crack it..." and hell did we crack it, while others were burning their asses off trying to remember the test for each salt, we were just cross-checking whether our decryption was accurate.

That day on, he was the master planner, be it bunking classes, lobbying in elections, and most of all trying to find a pattern in the question paper that the teachers set, believe me there always was a pattern, analyze the last 10 semesters' papers, and you can predict questions up to a certainty of over 80 percent (well yes, this is the reason we had good grades in the final few semesters). However, finding the pattern for questions was a tough deal, and yes, we were not successful in the first few attempts, but we kept trying, the stakes were high; by finding an accurate pattern, just imagine the number of hours we actually saved.

"Chal saale samose khilata hu, tu bhi kya yaad rakhega" Yadav wanted me to drag me out of my shell of depression.

"Saale DK Bose mere rejection ka party mana raha hai?"

"Khana hai to chal nahi to room pe baith ke 'hila'". Yadav was a character.

"Oye Silti chal" Yadav called for Shantanu.

"Ruk buddhe aa raha hu" came a prompt reply from Shantanu.

There we were, the entourage headed towards Bijoy da's canteen, our release point during moments of disaster and happiness alike. Days were passing by swiftly, companies were coming and going while I was appearing and getting rejected day in and day out. I could not have been more dejected with myself, getting into an NIT guarantees you one thing if not more, and that is a job. I remember how my neighbors greeted my parents saying "Bachcha NIT me chaala gaya hai, naukri to ab pakki hai, this is the beauty of IITs and NITs, you are guaranteed a job the moment you take admissions." This thought made me all the more tensed; how would I face those people who had such high hopes with me (at least I thought that they cared for me).

With every passing day, I was getting buried deep into self-hatred and guilt. I wish I could just end the agony, but along with this thought came the images of my parents, their hopes attached to me. If I kill myself they'll be shattered. I was holding on to it, but my situation went from bad to worse with every passing moment. I buried myself in my den and stayed there, I didn't speak to anyone, I was in an emotional hell. I so wished someone read my thoughts without me having to spell it aloud.

It is surprising how some people understand your mental situation. You don't speak a word, and yet there they are totally in sync with your frame of mind. These someone are called friends, and I was lucky enough to have a host of these guys.

In the hostel, you may get beat up by your seniors, you may have to do their odd jobs, you may have to serve them with an occasional cup of tea, but in the end, you get something delightful, something worth cherishing, something worth killing for; you get true friends, those who will stand by you in all walks of life.

Much has been said regarding "Unity in Diversity," and we all know what it is. But there is something that a hostel ragged guy would understand, and it is "UNITY IN ADVERSITY." When you face adverse situations together, your camaraderie goes up to a completely different level. Ever thought how army men are able to put friends before self? Well, I guess you know now.

My batch mates were no different, they could go to any extent to help their friends, and luckily I was their FRIEND.

I can't help but recall the moment when three guys, GKD, Paliya, and Rinku, came to my room and sat on my bed. I knew I was up for something special, you hardly saw this group together; these guys were always busy in their gaming world and came out of it only in dire situations. Situations like going to college to write a test, to meet the dean in case of attendance shortage etc, nonetheless never had come a situation where these guys were found wanting. They were always ready with a witty reply and a solution that would bail them out of any trouble. They were THE guys.

I knew they were here to discuss "me," but I was too sullen to start off the conversation so GKD started. Normally he was one of the most soft-spoken and mild-mannered guys. I distinctly remember his opening line.

"Bhosdike kyu chudwa raha hai apna life, why the hell are you doing this to yourself." The words were harsh, but the tone as mild as it could get.

"Saale aise ro dho ke kaha se kuchh hoga be, tu khud soch, you are an NITian boss, have some respect for yourself." He did

have a point, but again it is easy for someone placed in IBM to blurt these things, isn't it?

Before GKD could complete his sentence, Paliya jumped in:

"Dekho Ajeeet (even in this situation I couldn't help but notice the stretched "eee") ye naukri to lagni hai definitely lagegi, magar uske peechhe tum khud ko bhula rahe ho... Thoda prepare karoge to ho jaega koi dikkat nahi hoga, tum haar mat maano, we will help you in every possible way."

I was too depressed to react to this statement. Did he think that I was not preparing well? Actually, I had reached a stage in depression where I wasn't able to accept anything that even remotely suggested a shortcoming in me. Naturally, I did not take this remark positively. Assuming that these guys were taking turns trying to talk some sense into me, I turned towards Rinku. "Bol tu bhi bol kuchh. Say something."

"Mai kuchh bolne nahi aaya hu, batane aaya hu samjha SENAPATI," (Ranawat had a special knack of calling people names; I was SENAPATI because I used to strategize and execute the assaults on my professors).

"Tu job deserve karta hai ye tujhe kyu lagta hai?" believe me at this moment I felt a strong urge to break this little prick's nose, how dare he ask such a question? "Behenchod kya soch raha hai? kal bataega kya?" He meant business here.

"Abe tu khud dekh mera performance second year ke baad se. Har teacher ko thok ke rakha hai maine."

"First year me kyu nahi thoka? Us waqt pichwaare me dum nahi tha?" He better have a good point else he was in some serious problem, I thought.

"Abe first year me mere me itna confidence nahi tha, knowledge tha magar confidence nahi tha, bol tera point kya hai bhosdike?" I was yelling on top of my voice.

"You have made my point SENAPATI"

Ranawat's remark had made me really angry, and I wasn't in a place where I could analyze what I was saying; I was just yelling the words that came to my mind.

Ranawat continued:

"Yaar tu soch tera sabse strong point electrical machines, power systems, ya koi aur subjects nahi hai. You may be very good in these but tera USP tera confidence hai be. Saale tera confidence dekh ke kisi ki bhi phat ke haath me aa jaati thi. Tere ko agar naukri chahiye to ek hi upay hai be, rediscover the old Ajit, behenchod koi bhi situation aata tha tu kabhi ghabrata nahi tha be. Aur abhi dekh hum log tere ko samjhane aaye hai. Boss this is really sad." Finally what he said made sense to me.

"Yaad hai 2nd year ki baat" Ranawat sensing the effect of his words continued "Mere ko SKG (Satish Kumar Gupta) ne back de diya tha, tune kya kaha tha mere ko 'kisi me itni aukaad nahi hai joki tujhe rate kar sake. You are successful as long as you yourself don't think otherwise', why are you letting those people decide that you are a loser. You are not a loser to us; I hope you realize this too." Man I was moved, seriously I was now starting to think positively about myself.

"Chal ab sutta pila behenchod gala sukha diya tune" Ranawat laughed. This was expected; after all, we were NITians, and we cannot remain serious for long. We had a good smoke, a healthy laugh, and then they walked out, and with them walked out the gloomy, self-doubting, and a sobby Ajit.

The memories brought tears to my eyes. I put out the cigarette and started thinking about how things had turned and turned for bad. I was getting a healthy take-home salary, the incentives were great, I had my life covered, and I was on the verge of getting an on-site opportunity, something that every software engineer dreams of. Things seemed to be rosy, or at least they should have been. But somehow I was not able to feel the happiness that these things were supposed to bring. There was a void in my life that held me back. Amidst all the materialistic glory that I was provided with here, I was longing for something else - something more meaningful, something to add significance to my life. I was in a real pathetic state of mind.

Had I not always wanted this? Did I not sacrifice the fun and frolics of the final semester to get a job? Did I not spend those lengthy hours digging deep into books when I could have enjoyed with my friends instead? I was beginning to feel an unprecedented emptiness in my life. The things that I thought would bring happiness to my life were rendered useless, and the reason for that: I did not have anyone to share my moments with. I was lonely in a city of over 12 million people. How I wish I had someone to share my thoughts with, to go around partying on weekends, to enjoy the movies, or to simply lay back and enjoy a cup of coffee all by ourselves, without any stress, without any pressure, without dwelling over the complexities of life. How I wished my friends were here.

My train of thought was broken by my beeping phone. I was expecting another message from one of the fellow PZ-live'rs. I took the phone out, and what I saw surprised me.

Actually, the word "surprised" would be an understatement; I could not help but stare at the screen. “New message from Poorvi” it read. This was when I realized how long she had been off my radar. My heart rate increased. I started sweating. SHE had messaged me, Poorvi - the love of my life! She remembers me even after all these years, after all the events that transpired between us in the last 2 years.

“I don’t want to hear from you, EVER!”. Those were the last words she had said to me, and believe me, we did not hear from each other again. What could be the reason, why would she want to establish contact with me again? Could it be that she wants to get back with me? But again if she wanted that she would have done it years ago and not today. Another possibility could be that his message may not be for me, it could be for someone else, maybe somehow it got delivered to me. Even this hypothesis did not make much sense; she did not have my number, so the message getting delivered accidentally to me was out of the question. How did she get my phone number? A flurry of questions came rushing. My mind was cluttered with questions: what? Why? How? All questions, no answers. I read the message; it said:

"Hi Ajit!! How's life?"

Well, at least one thing was confirmed now; it was meant for me. However, there were a lot of questions that still remained unanswered. What was she doing texting me? And how did she get my phone number? I went through the text one more time, "Hi Ajit how's life?" Honestly speaking, I was a tad disappointed. I went through the message over and over again, trying to find meaning in an otherwise simple and straightforward question.

Why would a girl who cut all ties two years ago suddenly send this kind of message? There must be more to it than those words. At least that's what I wanted to believe. The thought of the possible reasons that might have prompted her to text me brought a smile to my face which wouldn't leave. The sorrow of losing her and the anguish of living without her for so long seemed to vanish in an instant. My heart was filled with indescribable ecstasy.

Her image flashed before my eyes, it had been two years since I had last seen her.

She seemed like a queen - high and regal. She had dark wavy hair, strikingly deep brown eyes, blood-red plump lips, with a natural rose blush on her pale and lightly freckled face, and this porcelain face, that seemed, if anyone had tried to hit it, it would break into a million pieces. Her smile was the most beautiful thing on earth, it started small but as it grew, it pressed her rosy cheeks up and slowly revealed her teeth, like a perfect pearl necklace. Finally, the smile reached her eyes, lighting them and causing them to crinkle at the corners.

She was by far the most beautiful woman I had ever seen. My God, she was beautiful.

How could I have not tried to get back with her? All those wonderful days we had spent together came flashing before my eyes. As I began thinking about it, my vision blurred. Everything around me turned hazy. Then, quietly, a little tear rolled down my cheek, and I felt a lump forming in my throat. Things were so good when we were together. I could hear her laughter and see her beaming smile before my eyes. I would have done anything to make her happy.

I was lost imagining her beauty when I realized that I had not replied yet. I recollected myself and typed, "I'm good. What about you?" That was all I could think of at that moment. We exchanged around thirty texts that day. Things finally seemed to be going good.

As if it was a routine, I took my phone out and texted the latest developments to my fellow PZ-Live'rs,

"Bhaiyau, guess who messaged me, Poorvi after nearly two years. Bahut khush hu yaar, don't know how to react."

"Congrats SENAPATI. Wo tere liye hi bani hai, ab tu kuchh chutiyapa mat kar baithna," replied Ranawat.

"Sahi hai be Ajit, maine kaha tha na tujhe sachcha pyar hamesha jeetta hai, really happy for you man," replied Suman.

Of all the replies that I received, one particular message made me really happy. It was from Shantanu, the master planner, "Sun bhai congrats be, these are some real good signs. Iss baar achchha hoga. One more thing I'm coming to Mumbai tomorrow. Milte hai, we'll kick some real Mumbaikar ass... what say dude..."

The prospect of meeting Shantanu after nearly two years cheered me up. He was one hell of a company. I got out of bed and headed for my customary shower before dinner. The bathroom stunk, and the iron in the water did not help my hair fall. But nothing could spoil my mood now. I was back in touch with Poorvi, and now Shantanu was coming to Mumbai.

I woke up the next day feeling particularly upbeat. I could not help but think about how things can turn around and how it's important to keep going in life and not let drawbacks or setbacks pull you down. You never know what the next moment has in store for you.

The best part of yesterday was "SUCKY," and I could not emphasize the words "SUCKY" more. Then suddenly, in one moment, life seemed to be perfect again. I was seeing everything in a completely different light today. It may sound clichéd, but everything around me seemed to be vibrant, more colorful, and more joyous. Somehow, the grass looked greener.

I was preparing to go to the office; it was the same place which just yesterday was the last place I would have wanted to be in. But today, it not only seemed to be cheerful, but I was also kind of looking forward to going there. I was happy, and there was nothing that could've brought me down.

I walked into the office, and everything felt great. If my manager happened to show up right now, I would have given him a big hug, the 'jaadu ki jhappi,' and told him that everything would be fine. I walked straight to my station, switched on my monitor, and started reading my morning newspaper.

"Good morning, Ajeete," Anjali wished me. Now that I was on the road towards getting back together with Poorvi, my attraction towards Anjali seemed to have fizzled away. I saw her in a completely different light today, probably the same way she saw me for the past year and a half, and it felt good to finally be able to see her as a friend. There was no guilt in my heart now.

"Good morning, Gappu..." I replied with a big grin on my face. "Gappu..." She said and started laughing. I don't know how, but I really called her "Gappu." Most days, I am a calculated person, and whatever I say, I weigh it in my mind at least twice before actually saying it. But today, it selemed as if I was drunk. Actually, I was drunk on happiness, ecstasy, and life altogether.

"Bas yaar... I don't know, aise hi bol diya, don't mind," I replied. "Arre, there is nothing to mind; it's kind of sweet," she replied with a smile that looked genuine. "Nisha aa jaae phir we'll go and have breakfast," Anjali said and went towards her station.

After a while, Nisha came. I greeted her with a smile and the customary "good morning." She kept her bag, and we headed to the cafeteria for breakfast. We ordered our usual and started eating. I had just taken the first bite when Nisha said, "Ajit... our manager has been replaced, suna kya?"

This came as a big surprise to me; on most other days, I wouldn't have given a damn about what happened to him, but today, I felt bad, kind of sorry for him. "Actually, I am really sorry to hear this, kal thoda panga hua tha, but..."

"Chal... kuchh bhi," Anjali did not buy that I was genuinely going to miss him.

"Arre, chhodo bhi, pata hai kaun hai naya manager apna?" Nisha said.

"Kaun hai? Who is he?" both me and Anjali asked this in unison.

"Srini..." Nisha said with a smile, as if they knew this person from before.

"Kya baat kar rahi hai... Are you serious? Great yaar," Anjali was not able to conceal her excitement.

"Arre kaun hai ye Srini? Hume bhi batao, even I want to be excited," I said.

"He was our team lead when we had first joined this project. He is really cool, one of the best leads I've ever seen," Nisha said.

"Chalo dekhte hai, let's see how cool he is," I said after finishing our meal.

I was looking forward to meeting this person; I was hoping he was as good as Nisha and Anjali were projecting him to be. We walked back towards our workstation, and as we did, I couldn't help but picture the scene from yesterday: My manager standing with that dreaded expression. Now, how things have changed; I was no longer angry or upset. Instead, I was on cloud nine for obvious reasons. I slowly went over to my place and started preparing myself for the day's work.

I had just started when I got a ping from a certain 'Jai Srinivas.' It said: 'Hi Ajit, please come to room number 403, have something important to discuss.' I was a bit confused initially; who was this 'Jai Srinivas' guy? I had never heard this name before. I checked the name again – 'Jai Srinivas.' It was then that it struck me, 'Srini' was short for 'Srinivas.' That message from Srini left me mighty confused.

I started to put two and two together. Yesterday, I had an argument with my manager, today he is replaced, and the person who replaced him wants to have a chat with me. All these things put together did not paint a good picture. Whatever the picture was, I still had to go see him. Sensing there was no escaping it, I strapped on a pair and walked towards his office.

"Oh, hi Ajit, please come," he greeted me cordially; this settled my nerves a bit.

"I'm Srini, your new line manager," he added.

I couldn't help but notice the way he prefixed a 'Y' to my name. I was always amused at how people from South India (especially from Andhra) prefixed a 'Y' to every word starting with a vowel. It's true, you can check, for example: "egg" becomes "yegg," umbrella becomes "yumbrella," ant becomes "yant."

"Yes, sir... I came to know about it this morning," I replied after a small pause.

"Oh then there was no need for that introduction," he said this with a smile.

I just smiled in response.

"I called you for a reason, actually we are planning to start our office in Bangalore, and I want you to fly there along with Nisha and Anjali," he said. This was not what I was expecting, but still, it was better than the other things I was contemplating.

"Okay, sir... when do we have to fly?" I asked.

"Tomorrow," he replied.

"But sir, tomorrow, isn't this a bit sudden?" I tried to reason with him.

"Yai yunderstand, Ajith. But there yis litttle yai can do. You have to leave tomorrow; you can leave early yand prepare for the journey." He left me no choice, he didn't spell it out, but he clearly meant there was no room for discussion here.

"Yand yes, don't forget to collect the tickets before you leave, yits yat the reception," he added as I left his room.

Actually, I didn't need the time to 'prepare' for the journey; packing my stuff would hardly take half an hour. I thought I could use that extra time to arrange for Shantanu's welcome.

I came back to my seat; I was supposed to leave in the second half. There was still some time left before I could leave for the day. I decided to take up some work, but I wasn't able to concentrate. So much had happened in such a little time that it was hard for me to grasp it all. I was really looking forward to Shantanu's visit. He was a guy who could easily brush off his aura of nonchalance.

Chapter 3

FRIEND IN TOWN

Later that evening, I went over to the kitchen to check the stock of liquor; two bottles of Carlsberg. Even though we were not much of a drinker, I knew two bottles wouldn't suffice. I had to order some more, knowing Shantanu's taste in drinks I ordered a carton of 'Heineken,' one of his favourites. After the necessary arrangements were made, I headed for a quick shower.

Ever since I received that text from Poorvi, I couldn't get her out of my mind. I was determined to make things work this time around. I clearly remember the final confrontation we had.

"Ajit, I am not being angry, but remember one thing, only CHEAP guys get drunk and call girls at night."

When I called her, she hung up, saying "I don't want to hear from you, EVER!"

My customized ringtone for Shantanu, "Shantanu calling! Shantanu calling!" brought me back to reality.

"Saale kaha marwa raha hai, aadat nahi chhuta hai tera. Kabhi to time pa aa jaya kar saale. I've been waiting for you for the last forty mins!!!" Shantanu was blasting away at me. It was then that I realized how long I was in the shower. I slipped into a T-shirt and jeans and rushed to the airport, battling the traffic to reach there in just under thirty minutes.

I looked around, trying to find the 'man.' I saw him standing in a secluded corner all alone with earphones plugged in.

That was Shantanu, he had not changed, he was the same person who had walked out of college two years ago. I could've bet he was listening to some sufi songs. He greeted me in an all-too-familiar hostel-style, "Madarchod baalau ka kya kiya be?" I was embarrassed; for two reasons. First, these words were not supposed to be used in public. College was different, but now we formed the 'respectable' class of society, and people looked up to us. Second, his remark about my balding head. I was too embarrassed to say anything. I just gave him a smile and hugged him.

"Samajh gaya samajh gaya, saale tu bada ho gaya lagta hai! Chhor, chal nikalte hai."

I was still stinging from the remark he had made earlier. I knew that Shantanu had sensed my embarrassment, and he too was embarrassed. But I did not make any effort to make him feel better. I helped Shantanu load his luggage into the cab that I had already booked and headed towards my flat in Vikhroli.

"Aur bata kaisi chal rahi hai zindagi?" I said, trying to strike up a conversation.

I had never imagined that things would become so awkward between us that we would need a conversation starter in order to break the ice. Maybe I was at fault. I shouldn't have reacted the way I did to his statement. Maybe he was just trying to be playful, bring hostel back into our lives. Back in college, no one would have thought that I would have reacted this way. In college, I used curses more than I used punctuation, and now I was pretending to be someone I was not.

"Kuchh nahi be, office ka kaam tha to socha ek din pehle nikal leta hu, tujhse milna bhi ho jaega. Tu bata."

"Abe mere ko bhi kal Bangalore jaana hai be, behenchod boss ne maar li." I was making an effort to make up for my earlier reaction.

I knew I did not have to apologize for him to understand that I really was apologizing. In a way, I was glad that I could be in 'hostel mode' for some time.

"Kaun si teri biwi hai yaha pe jo tension le raha hai. Kahi bhi bhej de jab tak shadi nahi hui hai, aaram se chale jaenge," he replied.

We had a lot of catching up to do, and the slow-moving Mumbai traffic gave us ample time to talk. He was in a relationship, recently received a good hike, and yes, he now had a steady girlfriend. There was nothing much that I had to share with him, or at least I did not want to do it in the cab. We reached my flat in around half an hour or so.

He went in to freshen up. Meanwhile, I ordered some chicken fries.

"Oye, you had said something about Poorvi, bol kya chal raha hai," he asked, drying his hair.

"Abe kuchh nahi be, she messaged me yesterday." I tried to avoid divulging the details, but I knew he would not let it go.

"Sahi chutiya hai be tu, you never said anything about her back in college."

"Kya batata be, kuchh khaas nahi tha kehne ko."

Just as Shantanu was warming up, the doorbell rang, giving me some more time to play with him.

"That must be the chicken I ordered; I'll get it." I got the chicken and paid the delivery boy.

"Chal beer peete hai. You'll like this one. Heineken. Mast smooth hai be."

"Bhai mai tere ko chhorunga nahi, you know me, I'll not let it go, so just be out with it." I knew Shantanu would not give up.

"Sun bhai agar ek baar chalu kiya to you'll have to bear with me till the end," I cautioned.

"Just get on with it, chaat mat chutiye." Shantanu was as eager as ever.

Chapter 4

HOW I MET HER

“I was 12 years old when I first saw Poorvi, she was really cute and also quiet. Usko dekhte hi pyaar ho gaya be,” I told Shantanu as he tried to get comfortable on the couch, gulping down the beer.

"Good news was that we were in adjoining buildings, separated by a narrow footlane. Mai usko apni khidki se dekhta tha every evening chhupke, she used to be there on her window. I always thought she knew I was looking at her, but she never said anything."

"Sahi hai be SENAPATI matlab 'mere saamne waali khidki me'," joked Shantanu.

"Ha be keh sakta hai, but please don't mock me, sun pehle, before I get wasted on this beer. Magar mai usko bol nahi paya apni dil ki baat, there were two reasons for this, first being that I was too chicken to go and tell her and second that our families were not particularly fond of each other."

"Ye bata... how old were you at that time?" Shantanu stopped me.

"Bataya to sahi tere ko, I was twelve, why do you ask?"

"Because that is one of the most awkward ages, you are too old to act childish and cute and barge into someone else's house innocently and too young to actually stage a protest against the restrictions imposed." he explained.

"Exactly, then probably you'll understand why I could not tell her how I felt."

"Tell me one more thing how old was she at that time?"

I could not understand why he was suddenly so interested in everybody's age.

"She was 9, actually approaching 10... Magar tujhe hua kya hai? Age kyu puchh raha hai. I feel as if I am sitting with a lawyer here."

"Abe agar tu usko us waqt bata deta how you felt to bahut maza aata kasam se, really, it would have been interesting," Shantanu was laughing.

"kyu bhai? Aisa kya hota?" I didn't quite understand what he meant.

"Sahi chutiya hai be tu, do you think that she was mature enough to understand what love meant? What do you think she would have done had you told her 'I love you'? She would have gone running to her parents and complained. Aur tuhi bata raha hai ki tum donau ke family relations kuchh khaas sahi nahi the. Now just imagine the scene had you told her how you felt."

"Sahi bol raha hai be, I am glad I waited and did not tell her straight away," I agreed with his reasoning.

"Chal aagey bata, how long did this go?" Shantanu started gulping down from the pint.

"Abe aaram se pi saale, you'll throw up," I cautioned him.

"No, I won't... tu ghabra mat, I won't soil your fancy place," He replied.

I wouldn't be completely honest if I said that I wasn't worried about the place getting soiled. Bottom shots almost always induce vomiting. But again there is no point worrying about these things when you are hosting a booze party. So I resumed:

"Will you believe if I said that this 'Aankh michauli' between me and Poorvi continued for nearly three years."

"Kya mazaak kar raha hai be behenchod, you mean to say that 3 saal tak tune usko bataya nahi ki tu usko pyaar karta hai? Really disappointed, pura naam kharaab kar diya tune apna chhhhiiiiiii." I knew it was the alcohol talking.

This was the real fun of having alcohol, you get to see these 'over the top' reactions on topics that otherwise would pass as 'uninteresting'. However, I decided to humor him:

"Height hai be... Things had not changed in those three years. I still didn't have the courage to talk to her; the gap between our families had not bridged. One thing had changed for sure; my love for her increased to levels of insanity".

"Khair chhod, maanta hu ki mai chutiya tha, nahi bata paya usko. But that wasn't the real tragedy, the real tragedy was..." I paused to gulp a mouthful of beer. "that my dad got transferred".

"hahahhaha baaal ye to hadd ho gayi be, saale abhi tak 'I love u' bola nahi and the separation had started!!!!! aisa kaand tere saath hi ho sakta hai be hahahaha" I must say it was humorous, but his reaction was a bit too much, this confirmed that the beer had made its way into his system and it was controlling his words.

"abe sun, we had to shift base to Namchi a place 90 kilometres South of Gangtok, I was devastated. Abhi tak usko kuchh bata nahi paya tha aur ye situation aa gaya. I didn't know what to do. Behenchod kaha jaata kisko bolta, I was feeling really helpless."

"Abe samajh sakta hu tera condition" he tried to pacify me.

I paused for a second to make sure that he genuinely meant what he said and was not being sarcastic, well surprised as I was, he actually seemed genuine, however I continued:

"The worst part was that I had not expressed my love for her."

"Saale jaake bata dene ka na... Bhosdike kya gadha tha be tu," Shantanu was back to his normal insulting self, it kind of felt good, actually with your college buddies those were the kind of words that you expect and not the mushy, sympathetic ones.

"Abe kya kehta, 'Poorvi I love you, I had loved you for the past 3 years aur abhi tak kehne ki himmat nahi ho rahi thi. And yes one more thing next week mai jaa raha hu, so we may not meet again.' Is this what you are suggesting?" Midway through my sentence I realized I actually should have said that, I mean I should have taken the chance; however, it was all in the past, past that was way into the 'past'.

"Abe to kya? Don't tell me that you left Gangtok just like that"Shantanu's voice was staggering, he probably had too much alcohol way too soon, however his eyes said that he could not believe I left Gangtok without talking to Poonam first.

"Abe sun, ye sab 11 years purani baatein hai, lots of things happened after that. Uspe dhyaan de," I tried to bring Shantanu in sync with the fact that this narrative was from the past. I could do nothing about it.

"11 years purani baatein my ass, the point is tune galat kiya tha, ab wo 11 saal pehle kiya ya phir aaj kiya, it still remains a mistake. And given an opportunity I would have had you castrated for this." Castrated? I thought that was a bit too much, but again he was not in his senses, he was expressing the superlative side of his emotion I decided to let him have this one, I humored him instead.

"Theek hai mere bhai galti ho gayi maaf karega?" I asked for his forgiveness, thinking it would pacify him.

"Bhai itna gussa mat kar, just think of my condition, just think what I was going through... anyway just let me continue."

"Finally the day arrived; we were supposed to travel that evening. I distinctly remember that last day. I was putting the last batch of our households in the truck when she walked past me with her younger brother, dressed in a velvet skirt and a cream-colored top, she looked like an angel if there was any." I paused for a second, walking down the memory lane made me nostalgic, that image of her is one the few memories that is still fresh in my mind. I was feeling the pain of separation all over again.

"Ab royega kya chutiye?" this is how we consoled each other, for us words were not important what really mattered was the underlying emotion.

"Any way, we started our journey, bidding good bye to the people we knew. Abe mai to nikal gaya tha magar peechhe kuchh important, bahut important cheez chhor raha tha. Pata hai worst cheez kya tha, the thought that she might never know how I felt about her." It seemed as if I had forgotten that things did not end there for me, I was feeling the pain that I had felt then.

"As the car started I looked out from the window, trying to get that one last glimpse of her, she was standing beside the narrow road looking as pretty as ever and this time our eyes met and she smiled, I couldn't believe this was really happening. I couldn't help but curse myself all this while she acted as if I never existed and the one time she actually noticed me was when we were relocating. I started crying there, I was crying at my misfortune; obviously, my parents thought I was crying because I would miss my friends." I recollected the time when me and Poorvi were separated for the first time, it might seem to be an exaggeration but I was feeling weepy so I stopped for a second to let the tears settle down.

"Abe... I can only imagine what you were going through." Shantanu said. There was no way that he could imagine what I was going through, if you've not faced it, you don't know it. But there was no point arguing with him. So I continued:

"I was looking out through the window; my heart was heavy with grief and eyes moist. I grew up in the hills so there was nothing spectacular about what I saw, it was just a routine drive with the river 'Teesta' flowing on one side of the road and on the other, there was this huge mountainous terrain, it was evening so the mist which had formed on the water was just beginning to float up. As we drove along we passed through a tea plantation, the field workers were preparing to leave for the day in their traditional Nepali dress with a basket hanging on their backs suspended from their forehead also being in the hills the clouds were low in fact if you looked out from the window onto the hills you could see them glide over the pine trees that covered the hills."

"Abe saale kya bol raha hai... just a routine drive... if this isn't spectacular then what is" I thought Shantanu would sense the sarcasm but he didn't.

"Abe gaandu, I was being sarcastic saale it was delightful, it would have been any traveler's delight, but I was too sullen to enjoy the thorough beauty of this place." I replied.

"We finally arrived at our quarters, it was a typical government facility with huge rooms, we had graduated from two-bedroom to a four-bedroom apartment and all the rooms were king-sized but no one seemed to be happy, it was understandable because my parents had never moved out of Gangtok in the last 19 years. People knew us there and now having to uproot our life was really hard on all of us, it was harder on me for reasons you already know." I said.

"Haa be... it must have been really difficult for you, but with all due respect I am least bothered about how big the rooms were and how your parents felt... tell me about Poorvi, kya kiya?" Shantanu did not like the way I was going in the depths, I was just trying to paint a picture but he probably did not want me to narrate it like a classical storyteller, he wanted the narrative to be on point.

"Ok as you wish... I started missing her like hell, pehle bhi usse mai zyaada baat nahi karta tha, still I used to see her every day. Now that she was not around her image did rounds in my head all I could see was her beautiful face, those lovely eyes, and the smile that made my heart skip a beat, it was as if I was in a dream and she was the only one in it." I paused to see Shantanu's reaction, he was gazing intently on the floor all this while probably trying to concentrate.

All that alcohol would have made it harder for him to understand all the things I wanted him to grasp.

"Abe tell me one thing, if you missed her like hell then why didn't you call her, like a man..." Shantanu asked, at least he was following the story.

"Well... for obvious reasons... Actually, not so obvious; I didn't have her number," I replied.

"Sahi hai be, phone number nahi tha, usse 100 kms door tha aur uske pyaar me bechain... How did you manage?" He asked.

"There was a friend of mine who had family ties with Poorvi's, maine usse maanga, magar us gadhe ne Poorvi ke ghar ka nahi uske shop ka number diya," I replied.

"Phir," Shantanu opened his second pint. I thought he was beginning to get interested in the story again.

"Maine us number pe call kiya and no prize for guessing, uske papa ne call uthaya, behenchod meri to phat ke haath me aa gayi."

"Abe sahi me? Call laga diya? Phir kya kiya be?" He asked.

"Kya karta, call disconnect kar diya... mer phat gayi uss waqt." I answered.

"Kya karta? Baat karta, kuchh to puchta..." He countered. I did not reply to this, I had nothing to add to what I had already said.

"Khair... jo bhi kiya wo ho gaya, its done ... Continue plz.... Oh sorry... ruk ek second ruk, sutta jalata hu, tu lega?" he held both the cigarettes between his lips and lit them together.

"Madarchod normally kyu nahi jalata hai be, saale college ki aadat gayi nahi hai abhi tak."

"Abe wo aadat hi kya jo badal jaae." Shantanu said, blowing smoke in the air.

"Chal ab shuru kar." he gave me the green signal.

I took the cigarette and continued:

"I was not able to talk to her, meri phat ke haath me aa gayi thi, all this while I was constantly cursing myself for being such a jerk. Magar it was water under the bridge, the moment had passed." Even today I regret that moment of weakness.

"Khair koi nahi, ab senti mat ho. eventually sab theek to ho gaya na ab frustu kyu ho raha hai?" I was a bit 'Senti' but I thought I had concealed it well enough; instead, he read right through me.

"Abe ghanta frustu ho raha hu, story sun." I retaliated.

"I called her at her shop one more time, this time I was determined that I won't screw it up, full confidence me bola 'Poorvi hai?' saamne se reply aaya 'ek second, de raha hu'... Behenchod.... Kya batau be aisi phati aisii phati ki kya batau kaisi phati... She came on the call and then I went cold... I froze, it seemed as if I had lost my power of speech." I was repeatedly showing how big a jerk I was back then.

"Phattu saala..." Shantanu remarked, as usual there was a sense of mockery in his voice.

"You know Shantanu sometimes something happens that reaffirms your faith that someone is present up there looking out for you."

"kyu aisa kya hua?" He asked.

"Just when I was losing hope of being with her again, one of the best things possible at that time happened; my dad was transferred back to Gangtok." I explained.

"Agar kisi cheez ko pure shiddat se chaho to saari kayanat usse tumse milane ki koshish me lag jaati hai." Shantanu was not a big Bollywood fan but he managed to quote the right thing at the right time.

"Ha yaar, pata nahi shayad upar waale se mera dukh dekha nahi gaya, barely two months and we were transferred back, this was the best thing that had happened to me for a long long time. We moved back and luckily the flat that we had vacated earlier was still available for rent, we promptly rented it, the owners were happy to have us back as their tenant and we were happy because this was a locality well known to us.

I was determined to not repeat the mistake I had committed earlier. Now I did not care what our families had for each other. I would befriend her. Enough of peeking around." I couldn't see myself, but in my head, it looked cool, saying something with attitude while gulping down the beer.

"That's my boy... but did you do something or was your resolve like this smoke which comes out all dense from your mouth but is lost in thin air after a while." Shantanu said releasing the dense white fog from his mouth.

"Ghanta, samajh ke kya rakha hai be tune mujhe?" I was not pleased at him saying what he said.

"Theek hai phir chal bata kya 'kiya' tune?"

"Abe mai pure josh me gaya uske ghar pe milne but things didn't work out the way I had planned..."

"Aisa kya ho gaya be" Shantanu was gearing up to mock me, he knew an opportunity would be presenting itself.

"Abe uske maa ne mana kar diya, ekdum plainly bola 'Kyu milna hai beta?' mai bhi mood me tha, bol diya, 'Bas aunty thoda personal baat karna hai'" I paused just enough to allow the situation to sink into his bloody head.

"Kya personal kaam hai, bhago yaha se, aaj ke baad kabhi yaha dikhe to halat kharaab kar dungi"

"Hahahaha gadhe saale kya keh raha tha, 'Now I did not care what our families had for each other. I would befriend her. Enough of peeking around' aur gaali kha ke aa gaya... hahaha saale sahi chutiya tha be tu, 'Bas aunty thoda personal baat karna hai' yaar kaun jo ladki ke maa se ye bolega be. Especially when you knew that she was not fond of you."

Well, he did have a point. It was highly naive of me to use that sentence; well, that is how I was back then.

"Bandhu have you heard the saying 'bad things happen in pairs', well mere saath aisa hi hua."

"Nothing unexpected, seriously had there been an award for screwing up you would have been the top contenders, alongside Ashish Nehra, of course." He was right, wasn't he? I mean I may not have been good enough to overhaul Nehra, but considering my run in the last few years, I was confident I could give him a run for his money.

"Ab soch kya raha hai? Bata na aur kya bura hua, tera screw ups sunne me bada maza aata hai be" the twinkle in his eyes showed that he was really enjoying my misfortune.

"Iss bar wo shift kar gayi!!!"

"Kya? Sahi me? Behenchod isse kela kehte hai be. Pehle tu gaya ab wo chali gayi. Ye bata how far was her new place from yours?" he asked.

"They had a rented accommodation pehle, and now they shifted to their own flat. And see their stupidity, they bought the new flat ekdum dur, matlab seher se dur. So until and unless I planned a visit, there was no way I could meet her." I cited my helplessness.

"Let me see if I am still with you, you loved a girl since you were 12 years old. Quietly stalked her for nearly 5 years, never spoke to her about your feelings, got transferred to a place 100 kms away, and when lady luck finally smiled at you and you came back, she moved away to a place where you could not see her anymore, to top it all you had not said the three words to her yet!!! God I'm loving your story."

He was mocking me, making fun of the fact that I could not tell how I felt about her; still, I was happy that he was following the story.

"Oye betichod saale aise mazaak na uda, I was in a real bad place back then, I could not go there to visit her, had we been friends then maybe... and now you are taking a dig at me. Not cool man... not cool." I voiced my dissent, I wanted him to know I did not like his mocking.

By now both of us were down 3 bottles, one of the effects of beer is that it makes you want to pee. Shantanu made the famous 'T' asking for the timeout, I let him go take the break, actually, the alcohol had started doing its thing on me. I was starting to feel sleepy, and now that Shantanu went for that break, I lied down on the floor to relax my body. He came back from the little timeout.

"Oye chutiye so raha hai kya? saale abhi tak to tu 'I Love U' pe bhi nahi pahucha hai. Aisa mat kar, uth be saale" Shantanu yelled.

"Ruk saale chal thoda bahar ghum ke aate hai, lagta hai chhadh gayi." I stood up, shaking my head, jerking it sideways, expecting to shake off the drowsiness.

"Sutta lena mat bhulna be" Shantanu shouted as I went into my bedroom to get my slippers.

"Bade din ho gaye be since we took a round together haina?"

I recalled how back in college we used to go out on long walks after dinner through the beautiful lanes puffing on a cigarette that had been on at least 4 lips. Breathing out dense the white fog of smoke in cold winter evenings was an experience of its own kind.

"Chal aage suna." Shantanu asked me to continue with my story.

"She was gone, but there still remained a ray of hope in an otherwise dead romance, her family had shifted their residence but their place of business remained the same." I tried to highlight the silver lining on an otherwise dark cloud.

"Abe, what were the odds that you would be able to see her. Khud soch probability kitni hai, pehle she has to come to her shop, secondly, you'll have to be there at the same time." Shantanu was one logical bastard. He always evaluated the situation based on all the possible outcomes.

He was right in his own logical way, but what he did not know was that love did not follow the rules of Physics or Maths. It has a mind of its own.

"Anyway, bata ki aage kya kiya tune?" he was eager to know how did I 'manage'.

"Like you said it really was difficult to see her, but I can't describe how I felt whenever I saw her. If I've ever been truly happy, it was during those moments. I used to do rounds of her shop, most of the days she wouldn't be there, but when she would be and I managed to get a glimpse of her, it would make my day."

"Now this had become a routine for me, I used to go out on rounds every evening, some days she would be there and on others, well, I wouldn't be so lucky."

"How long did this go?" Enquired Shantanu.

"Approximately a year." I answered, I knew I was up for some mocking.

"Are you some kind of a fool, if you're telling the truth, never say it to anyone else, no one will believe you. Saale chutiyau ke duniya me bhi ek limit hota tha be. But not now, you are the new benchmark, bloody asshole." Shantanu was furious with me.

"Abe I regret what I did back then. Things should have been handled differently."

"Chal aage bata."

"Kya kiya isse pehle kab kiya ye batata hu. Class 12 ka boards tha, I even remember the date, 6th Dec 2006. That day I went to get the application form for IIT-JEE. Like I always did, I crossed her shop and there she was sitting radiantly on the chair meant for the owner.

It's not that I had not seen her before, but something happened which I cannot describe, I had a strong urge to talk to her." I guess my face reflected the exact emotion which I had undergone.

"Saale, that explains the bad score in boards." Shantanu grinned, after a long time, I must say.

"I couldn't sleep the entire night; all I did was think about her. I felt the same restlessness I felt when I was in Namchi."

"Phir kya kiya? Call kar ke disconnect kar diya hoga." Not his fault again, he didn't expect me to do anything better.

"Abe nahi be, raat bhar to kisi tarah guzaara. Phir plan banane baith gaya. Actually, mere paas to uske shop ka number tha if you remember."

"Sahi sahi sahi, I hope tera plan 'Bas aunty thoda personal baat karna hai' se better tha" he was back to his humiliating self.

"Abe nahi, iss baar thoda bada ho gaya tha na so the degree of naivety kam ho gayi thi." I joked.

"Bata kya kiya?"

"I knew two things about Poorvi, first the name of the school she studied in and second, she had a penchant for writing. I had planned to get her phone number using this information." I added with a grin.

"I called up at her shop, uske dad ne uthaya phir pure josh me full on fluent English me bolna shuru kiya. 'Hello uncle I am Ajit the literary secretary of T.N.A (Tashi Namgyal Academy) and actually I need to talk to Poorvi regarding an article, I would be highly grateful if you could pass me her number,' the ploy worked big time. The next thing I remember was him dictating her daughter's number to me."

"Sahi hai be, matlab duniya me tere se bhi bada chutiya hai koi. Is tarah kaun phasta hai be, mazaak to nahi kar raha hai na?" Shantanu found it really hard to believe that this trick worked.

"phir kya kiya?"

"Gadhe... kya puchh raha hai be? Aur kya karta, call kiya usko, isn't it obvious what I would have done now that I had her number."

"Sorry..." he apologized.

"Kya bola that is a different issue, tu ye soch mera condition kya ho raha hoga. This was a girl I was in love with for the last 6 years. I never had enough courage to go and tell her how I felt." I explained my state of mind.

"Madarjaat ye bata call kiya ya nahi" Shantanu was really eager to know my development. To be honest, I had not thought that he would be so interested in my love life.

"Call to kiya magar meri aisi phati ki kya batau. Jaise hi call usne receive kiya meri to phat ke haath me aa gayi. I started blabbering 'No Ajit don't tell mat bol ajit, it's not right'." I recounted my experience.

"Hahaha sahi comedy be, maaki aankh teri, O be 'No Ajit don't tell mat bol ajit, its not right' sahi chutiyapa kiya be tune" he could not stop laughing. It seemed to be the most amusing thing he had heard. Again, who would blame him for this comic outburst?

"chal aagey bata kya kiya." he prompted me.

"Mai to aise hi hil raha tha. I was lost for words, phir usne initiative liya aur mujhe sambhala."

"Abe ye kaise hua be?" he was perplexed?

"Relax Ajit; even I am feeling the same thing. Don't be nervous, bol do." These were her exact words.

"I love you," I blurted out as if I was possessed.

"I love you too," she replied. I could distinctly hear her giggles. The way she said those words, you understood she seriously meant it.

"Abe shudurbhai (an Assamese slang) masti to kela (another Assamese slang). Sahi sahi sahi... finally after all the ups and downs it worked out." There was a gleam in his eyes; I had known him for over 6 years now, and one thing was for sure, he really meant it.

"Abe ab to raasta clear ho gaya tha na? Finally, you let Poorvi know how you felt about her. Aagey kya hua ye bata. Saale itne der se tere story me koi positive baat nahi aa rahi thi. Finally, kuchh achchha sunaya tune. Kudos to you, jaha panah tussi great ho, toffu kubul karo..." Shantanu did the trademark 3IDIOTS move; it was hilarious to say the least.

"Phir kya tha, I was over the moon, if you've ever been in love you'll understand. There does not remain a speck of negativity in you. You are somehow filled with an undescribable positive energy. Everything around you seems to be lively and vibrant. Mere shakal pe ek smile sa baith gaya tha permanently. Hamesha usi ke baare me sochta rehta tha." I was just going on and on. Those were the days when I was most jovial.

"Ek aur cheez be, the things that happened during that period stay with you for a long long time." I added.

"like?"

"During those days ek ad aaya tha pepsi ka 'pepsi cafechino'. It had Priyanka Chopra and Kareena Kapoor in it. Somehow that ad has remained with me all these years. Jab bhi I recall those days with Poorvi mujhe wo ad zarur yaad aata hai be."

"Seriously? Theek hai yaad rakhunga aur agar mere saath aisa nahi hua to teri lene pahuch jaunga." He said.

"Maar liyo saale, magar uske liye tujhe pyaar karna padega, saale college me bhi kabhi kisi ladki ke baare me baat nahi karta tha, mujhe to tere pe shak ho raha hai saale 4 saal boys hostel me raha aur ek bhi ladki se koi interaction nahi. I wonder how you landed Disha"

There we were, the NITian within us had woken. We showered each other with pleasantries for a good 10 minutes; it was so pleasant that I have decided not to include it in this piece of writing.

"Chal aagey bata kya hua? Love story ka the end ho gaya mat bolna" Shantanu wanted me to continue.

"Wo kehte hai na Pyaar andha hota hai sach kehte hai. I could have called her up anytime in the last 6 years. Magar nahi what time did I choose? ...board exams ke theek pehle."

"Sahi chutiya hai be tu. Jab pyaar ne dastak di tab tune call kiya. Aur kya padhai ki baat kar raha hai be. Pata hai kitna padhta tu. Baal pyaar ke baatau me padhai na ghusa gussa aata hai behenchod." For once I agreed with Shantanu.

"Sab sahi chal raha tha, we used to talk for hours, kabhi kabhi ghumne bhi chale jaate the. Since we wanted to conceal it, hume ye sab chhup chhup ke karna parta tha. Since it was boards time we did not get enough time to spend with each other. Kyuki ghar se bahar rehne ka kuchh bhi bahana banau 2-3 hours se zyada nahi reh sakte the."

"Tu ghar se permission leke nikalta tha?" Shantanu found it difficult to believe that I was so tied down back then considering how I was now.

"There was one more problem, we were from different states, I was a Bihari and she was a Marwari."

"So what's the big deal?" he was not aware of the social stigma I presumed.

"Big deal? Tell me one thing, of all the people in India if you were to pick one community that was hated the most, which one would you pick?" I tried to show a mirror to Shantanu.

"Well, beyond doubt its Biharis, for reasons I don't understand." I said as Shantanu was a bit apprehensive spelling the answer out.

"Naturally our families would not approve of this relation." I put the final bit of information before him.

"Khair... I assume things worked out well later on" he enquired.

"Well, we used to talk for around an hour every day, we had 'phone names' for each other, agar koi usse puchti ki kisse baat kar rahi hai to she used to say Pallavi, and if I was asked the same question I would say Amit."

"With all due respect Ajit isme batane layak kya tha, it sounds so gay" I wasn't expecting this remark from him.

"Abe chutiye it has a reason isiliye mention kiya, gaandu samjha hai kya mere ko?"

"I thought that Pallavi did not exist, it was probably a name that she had arbitrarily coined."

"Sahi me tu maha chutiya tha be, it is natural that she will mention a real person and most probably a person that is known to the family to eliminate further questions." he saw what I couldn't see.

"Ab phataphat ye bhi bata de ki kya chutiyapa kiya iss naam ko lekar?" Shantanu was sure that I must have screwed up.

"I remember the date 10th March 2006, next day Maths ka paper tha, and I was kind of certain that she was my lucky charm. I called her multiple times, only to find her sister on the other side of the call each time. I became restless, they rightly say, when in love you lose your ability to make rational decisions. I took a step I would regret for a long long time." I was feeling guilty for that even today.

"Abe jaldi bata kya kiya tune, maza aayega" he was eager to laugh his ass off.

"Abe chal room chalte hai pehle, bahut late ho gaya sutta bhi khatam ho gaya"

"Maa behen ek kar dunga teri saale bata kya kiya as we walk back" he wouldn't let it go.

"As I told you she would not receive the call, so I decided to talk to her sister and ask for her. Naturally she asked who I was, stupidity struck and I said PALLAVI. She wouldn't stop laughing, wondering why? Pallavi was sitting with her right there in their living room." I can't describe the way Shantanu laughed; such was the ferocity of his laughter that even Rajpal Yadav would have taken tips from him.

"Yes, she found out that you were not Pallavi, how was that so bad?" He regained himself before asking.

"Sasuri agar uski behen ye baat apne tak rakhti to naa, usne to pura broadcast kar diya."

"'Poorvi ko koi ladka call karta hai, jab maine uska naam pucha to usne Pallavi bataya' now tell Poorvi ka kya haal kiya hoga uske parents ne. She called me back and in very stern words said 'Ajit it was a really big mistake that I decided to befriend you, mai galti sudharna chahti hu, aaj se kabhi mujhe call mat karna'."

"So what were you expecting? Bolegi hi na... tune jo uski laga di thi. But she did not mean it, I hope tune kuchh react nahi kiya ispe" There he was giving his verdict on yet another point. He wasn't wrong, I must say.

"Abe yahi to galti kar diya maine, I didn't consider her situation, the pressure she must have been under at that time, maine usse hi bura bhala suna diya."

When I recalled this episode, I couldn't help curse myself for my juvenility.

"I am having a bad feeling, bata tune exactly kya bola?"

"Yahi ki 'mujhe bhi koi interest nahi hai TUJHSE baat karne me, if you consider that this was a mistake then rectify it and make sure that this is rectified forever'" I can't believe that I had used these exact words for her, what a fool I was, first I was at fault for getting her into trouble, then I had the audacity to utter these words.

"Tujhse bada gadha nahi hoga kahi pe, saale apni shakal dekhi hai, mujhe bhi koi interest nahi hai tujhse baat karne me'. Galti thi be ye, bahut badi galti thi."

"Khair ye hum logau ka pehla break tha." I added.

"I wasn't able to concentrate on my studies thereon, papers to dena pada, koi interest nahi reh gaya tha, kuchh bhi karne baithta tha, I used to end up imagining her. This was the girl I liked since I was little and somehow I managed to screw up this wonderful relationship with her within a month." I don't know what it was, but whenever I revisited the past I used to end up all sad and disheartened. It had more bad memories than good ones, at least on the Poorvi front.

"Abe lets skip the sad part ye bata ki wapas kaise manaya usko? How did things work out finally?" Shantanu saw the distress in my eyes; believe me alcohol really amplifies your emotions, both in your actions and your demeanor. All the drinkers would agree with me on this.

"Abe bhosmadike darwaza to kholne de be. Saala sab kuchh hil raha hai, ye le chabi tu khol." I handed the keys to Shantanu.

We entered the room it was the same room, it had the same walls, the same windows, same furniture. But there was something really different, there was a drunken guy willing to speak his heart out about something he barely spoke and there was another drunken guy who was willing to hear him. We sat down on the floor and lighted a cigarette each. I was feeling really light, don't know why, maybe because I was with a dear friend or maybe because I was speaking about Poorvi, whatever be the reason it was working wonders for me, I was having the most memorable crests and troughs of emotions that I've had in a long long time.

I continued my tale:

"Things were not going great, in fact, it was bad, really bad. I tried calling her up many times but all I could get out of her was, 'I've made it very clear Ajit, I don't want to talk to you anymore'"

"Yeah, you had hurt her real bad... but I thought she would have mellowed down by now" Shantanu added.

"Well clearly she hadn't 'mellowed' down, and believe me I had lost all hopes. I had given up on her. I had tried everything I could to get her to forgive me, but she did not."

"Don't be depressed now, saale. Ye past ki baat hai, ye depressing part chhod. Bata maamla theek kaise hua? How did it happen?" Shantanu wanted me to skip the part where I would get all emotional and take a sidetrack.

"Well, I got through AIEEE and secured a seat in NIT Silchar. Waha jaake kisike paas time tha be, it was as if we were at the mercy of the seniors. You know how it was, don't you? I got so engrossed in college life, and by college life I mean ragging, that I barely had time to even think about the day that just went by, let alone think about Poorvi. Remember how we used to wake up early in the morning to serve tea and fill bottles for our seniors, going to their rooms, asking for their cups and their bottles, standing in those long queues, and then finally delivering them back to their rooms... Abe, the funny part was when we used to spit in the bottles of those seniors who targeted us during mass calls... Ek senior ko to maine toilet ke tap se paani bhar ke de diya tha..." I started recollecting the past.

"Saale, teri yahi aadat mujhe achchhhi nahi lagti. Behenchod, tu track badal leta hai, and saale, itna descriptive kyu ho raha hai? Maine bhi wahi ragging face kiya tha, so get to the point." Shantanu was truly irritated.

"Abe, agar story sunna hai to waise hi sunna padega jaise main suna raha hu".

" Chal, theek hai, jaise sunana hai suna, but make sure that you complete it before sunrise."

I glanced at the clock, 2:23 am. We still had lots of time.

"Because of ragging, I had kind of forgotten Poorvi."

"Ragging?" Shantanu interjected.

"May not have been just ragging, might have been my stupidity too, but she was the one who would not receive my calls. She was the one who said that it was a big mistake, not me." I was having mood swings of my own; something had really worked me up. I was angry, very angry. There was just one problem, though; I didn't know who I was angry with.

I mean all this happened in the past, and I shouldn't be mad at the past.

"Theek hai, theek hai, aagey bata kya hua."

"You know that those days I had started following someone else in college."

"Abe ha... there was this girl, kya naam tha... haa be, even that is a story in its own class, real nice one at that too." I knew Shantanu was mocking me; he had witnessed the entire episode.

"Saale, mazaak mat uda be. I know I had done some really stupid things back then, but you don't have to rub my face in it, do you?" Shantanu's sarcasm really pissed me off.

"Height case hai be saale, mazaak kaha uda raha hu be, magar one clarification please, what did you see in that little girl?" Shantanu could barely conceal his amusement.

I must admit that my attraction towards her was a mystery to many. People could not decipher what it was that attracted me towards her. I am not saying that she was ugly or had some issues which made her unappealing. She was an average-looking girl with everything in place, but what she had, and most people neglected, was her immense literary talent. She was mighty talented; there was some X-Factor in her that drew me towards her. I saw her on the first day of college, and there was something about her that drew me towards her. Her plain white kurta kameez, round spectacles, hair neatly combed into a single plait, completed with a beautiful 'gajra' skillfully made out of mogras. The fragrance of the mogra was enchanting.

I saw her and smiled out of courtesy, which I later found out was not considered really courteous by the female folk of our college. However, she replied with the sweetest possible smile one which stayed with me for a long, long time and was immensely responsible for creating a wonderful first impression.

The first impression that she had made was not based on her talents. I mean, how is it possible for someone to discover all the talents of a person based on a single smile? I was no superhero. All I knew was that she was special, and as I got to know her, I was awed by the enormity of her talents. She was not one of those girls you find in engineering colleges who act like princesses just because they were girls. In fact, she was as rebellious as the most rebellious guy in college. She was never short of ideas when it came to doing something creative. She was always active and took a keen interest in organizing stuff, mostly literary. People did not get it, but whenever I saw her, she oozed confidence. To me, she was the ultimate girl who deserved respect. I was at fault because I did not realize when this respect towards her turned into attraction, the attraction that was not reciprocated, and I am not surprised why. It was this drive of attraction that made me do things I regret. She was the best girl I had seen, of course after Poorvi. Shantanu had witnessed each and every episode of this story with me; definitely, he was not interested in knowing what I saw in that 'Little Girl,' so there was no use explaining it to him.

"I saw nothing. I was probably blinded by the fact that I had recently lost a girl who had all the qualities that one could look for in a girlfriend, and also the fact that I was stuck in a college far, far away from home. Maybe that I was fed up with all the ragging and profanities showered upon me by my seniors."

"Theek hai re bhai, itna garam kyu ho raha hai? Just chill..."

"You are aware that I had been turned down by Sandhya. Things were getting gloomy for me again. Sasuri do-do ladkiyon se reject hua, ragging me koi respite nahi tha, and deep down I was still in love with Poorvi. Kitna bhi try kar leta, I could not get over her. She meant the world to me."

"Ya... it would have been really tough on you, but you two eventually worked out your differences and got together, wo bata kaise hua?" Shantanu asked.

"Abe, I shut myself down. Ragging period me to tujhe pata hi hai, there was no time to do anything else other than to follow our seniors' orders. I never gave myself any free time. If I didn't have time, how would I think about her, right?" I went into a trance, recollecting the old college days.

"Senapati, I like the details, but I would rather have you come to the point and ye bata ki Poorvi se contact kaise hua?" he was just not willing to listen to anything else than the exact story. I don't blame him; we had faced the music together, so there was no point telling him how it was back then.

"Chal, theek hai, sun to phir." I was annoyed by the constant interruptions.

"It was the first Sunday of August, the friendship day, and she called."

"Abe on friendship day? This can't be good."

"Kyu? Why is that?" I was kind of confused. How could that be a bad thing?

"Are you not aware of the globally recognized term 'just friends'? This is something that every single guy dreads. If you enter this zone, there is no escaping. You'll be branded a 'friend' your entire life," Shantanu explained.

"But it seems that nothing of that sort happened to you. Bata kya hua iske baad?"

"After that call, things started to improve. It looked like we were starting to find that old repo. I was treading really carefully this time around. I was determined not to screw up this time around. After a couple of weeks, she said that she wanted to meet me. This was an opportunity that I was not willing to let go of. It was in between our semesters, but I was not going to let this stop me."

"Kaha milne gaya tha, and please don't tell me that you went to Gangtok." I could sense the excitement in his voice.

"Nahi be, gadha samjha hai kya? We decided to meet in Kolkata. Mai to nikal gaya pure josh me. I did not give a damn about what college had to say regarding absconding. I was just delighted to meet the girl of my dreams. When the flight landed, all kinds of thoughts started coming. I had not been face to face with her in the last 7 months. I came out of the airport, and there she was. God, she looked beautiful. I can't describe how she looked. It seemed that an angel had descended, and now she was there waiting for me. I was the luckiest man on the earth. A girl as beautiful as her standing to greet me. What more could I have asked for?

Just then I realized that she was my girlfriend now. How should I greet her? Should I hug her, place a peck on the cheeks, kiss her passionately, or just shake her hands? My heart started pounding faster with every step that I took towards her. The smile that I had worn while deboarding the plane, the smile which grew a thousand times more faded quickly when I saw her. With those thoughts doing rounds in my head, I crossed the barricade. As I took the final step out of the cordoned area, she came running towards me and wrapped her arms around my neck. It was one of those moments that make you forget about the world, inhibitions, and the various restrictions imposed by society. You care about no one but the person who is in your arms and your feelings towards that person. It's that feeling with which you can live the rest of your life. Believe me, Shantanu, there is no better feeling than this. Just imagine how you would feel when your presence is embraced by the person that you care for the most in your life." My heart started knocking against my ribs as I relived the past. I felt the same ecstasy that I had felt back then. The only difference being that today I was recollecting that moment instead of living it.

"Baal... sahi romantic situation tha be." He was genuinely enthusiastic about this. You can tell whether or not an NITian is faking by the choice of his words.

"How was the flight, Mr. Engg?" Poorvi said with a grin, almost teasing me.

"It was an ugly spat, right?" I heard what I said as I spoke. Of all the things that I could have said, I chose to say this, this to break the ice. Could there be anyone stupidier than me? I mean here I am meeting a girl, my love, after almost a year, and this is what I had to say, reminding her how things ended the last time we were together.

"Ya, it was bad... nobody's fault." I couldn't help but appreciate her temperament. I had gone through this moment hundreds of times in my head, rehearsing exactly what I would say and how I would say it. I had rehearsed every minute detail possible. But now when the moment finally arrived, I was left fumbling for words.

"Sahi hai be saale usne poocha how was the flight, and you replied it was an ugly spat... hahahah baal tere se kya expect karu, just when I think ki tu chutiyape ke peak pe pahuch chuka hai, you outdo yourself." It would be unfair if I blamed him for his mockery.

"Sahi behenchod hai be tu. Khud to ladki ko dekh ke phat jaati hai teri, sahi se baat tak nahi kar paata hai tu. Mujhe gyaan dene chala hai patti insaan." Shantanu was always awkward with girls, maybe his 'all boys schooling' was responsible for this.

"We spent the day together, went around the city. That was the first time I had been to a metropolitan. I'd be lying if I said that I wasn't awestruck by the enormity of the town. Everything was so grand and magnificent. Well, the city was beautiful, but I couldn't take eyes off her beautiful face. The glaze of the setting sun was reflecting from her marble-smooth skin. She slowly raised her dupatta seeking some shade. The crimson of the setting sun on her glistening skin painted a picture-perfect scene. The way she flung the end of the dupatta over her face completed the spectacle.

"Stop it... gir jaoge..." She said playfully, punching me. Her image was paving its way directly to my heart through the eyes.

I took a quick glance at my wristwatch; it read 3:30. I had a flight to catch in the morning, and Shantanu had to go to the office, but the renaissance had made every thing else take a back seat, things that would have had a priority otherwise had taken a backseat somewhere. Right now, both me and Shantanu were in a different world. I was in a world where I could see Poorvi's face distinctly, could sense her beauty. About Shantanu, I'm not sure. All I know is that he was also somewhere, and that somewhere was definitely not here. It had been a long, long time since I had a night out. Today was different; meeting a college buddy made me forget about the present; I was reliving the past, the glorious past.

I looked at Shantanu; he was lying on the floor, an empty bottle of beer by his side, and some cigarette stubs. Clearly, he was sleepy.

"Abe saale tujhe neend aa rahi hai? 3 bottle aur bachi hui hai. Khatam karna hai." To be honest, I was feeling equally sleepy.

"Chal ek ek bottle kholte hai, baaki ki story daaru ke saath," I suggested; actually, my throat was parched with all the storytelling. Both of us fumbled to find the bottle opener, but it wasn't there, not at least at arm's length.

"Opener ke maa ki aankh, I will open the damn bottle with my teeth." We, NITians, had this funda that whenever someone starts blabbering in English, it means that person is drunk. Well, we were both drunk and fatigued.

This fatigue was in no way going to deter the jolly mood I was in. I was happy because I was reliving the moments that I had spent with Poorvi; there was, however, a speck of disappointment because I was 'reliving' that moment and not 'living' it. I imagined how I would be looking right now, beer in one hand, cigarette in the other, with Poorvi's image in mind. I must have made a perfect portrait of 'Devdas.' These random thoughts of mine were broken when Shantanu spoke, and he spoke the same thing that he had been saying all evening.

"Chal aagey bata." I continued:

"Finally, the sun set, and the artificial lighting took over; the luminous covering over the city was captivating, and some cheap food joints were decorated in such a way that it gave you a sense of festivity."

"Abe samajh gaya Kolkata bahut sundar tha, aur tu bahut bada chutiya. Saale mai apna neend Kolkata ke baareme sunne ke liye nahi barbaad raha hu. Apni story suna re..."

This type of deviation from the main track is common when your blood has been contaminated by a substantial amount of alcohol, and actually I was just trying to paint a mental picture for him, but he did not seem to be interested.

"Everything was fine till we finished taking the tour of the city. We walked around, arm in arm; at times she would rest her head on my shoulders, and when she did that, it felt great, fabulous, in fact."

"So when did it begin to be 'not fine?'" Shantanu inquired.

"We finished roaming and headed towards our hotel. We had booked two different rooms. I was conflicted, really confused; my heart wanted me to spend maximum time with her, but my head did not agree. Things should not be rushed. With these conflicting thoughts, I walked towards the hotel room." Shantanu stood up, his face lit up in anticipation. There was a mischievous smile on his face.

"Kya kiya ye bata?"

"Abe dimag ka har logical part mere ko bol raha tha alag lag room book kiya hai, let it be that way. Agar saath raat guzaara to things will end up being complicated. Then I glanced towards her; she was staring at the floor while walking. She too was confused, about the same thing I assumed. Abe uske chehre pe jo look tha na, kasam se pagal bana diya... Dimaag gaya tel lene, uska wo look mai describe nahi kar sakta, intensely gazing the floor, nervously biting her nails. She was everything a man would want and more." Shantanu clutched my arms and 'dhwwwaaaaaappppp' gave a slap on my back and yelled 'WISHHH Kelaaaaa.' This was a unique way of displaying affection. I didn't mind it; alcohol served as a good anesthetic.

"We reached the lobby; it was late still I invited her for a cup of coffee. Hesitatingly she agreed. She walked into the room nervously. I myself was a nervous wreck but tried my best to mask it. The room was decently funrnished with a king-size bed and a couple of chairs.

We sat on the bed side by side; to say that we were nervous would have been an understatement. This was the moment I had dreamed of for years. She was the person

I had been in love with for over 7 years, and in those 7 years, I could just imagine how it would be to talk to her. Up until last year, it seemed like a distant dream to even talk to her, and now I was sitting with her on the same bed."

"Kasam se re bhai... when you had started telling the story, this was the last thing I imagined would happen, after all the chutiyapas, you finally had your day... Finally tera bhi din aa hi gaya. This confirms at least one thing, every dog has his day, sorry for the interruption, Please continue." He was mocking me... but I did not mind it.

Slowly but assuringly I placed my hand over her's. Even though we had been walking all morning together holding each other, this felt different, different in a good way. She shyly took her hands away, I waited for a couple of seconds and then made another attempt, this time I was firmer. I held her hands and looked into her eyes, she was trying to avoid direct eye contact, and there was a hint of shy smile on her face. 'Chhoro na, kya kar rahe ho?' She said but there was no real resistance, I knew she did not want me to stop. Her shy demeanour made her all the more irresistible. After some persuasion she turned towards me and looked straight into my eyes, the shyness that was there in her eyes just a few moments back was gone; there was an intense look in those eyes. The look that said she wanted me then and there. I leaned in and reached out for her lips, she kissed me back. I started off by kissing her lower lip. I had held her head with my left hand and wrapped my right hand around her waist. I completely sunk into her.

I was recollecting the time which I had spent with her, there was no way that I would've divulged the details to Shantanu, and even though he was a dear friend it was 'unethical' to speak about that moment with someone else.

"Kaha kho gaya be?" Shantanu brought me back to reality.

"Arre kahi nahi... bottle pass kar." I said, deflecting the original question...

"Abe agle din kya hua, I bet things would have been really awkward for you two..." I was surprised and equally glad that he did not intrude my space.

"Next morning I woke up with Poorvi next to me, this was like a dream come true. She was still asleep, looking as peaceful as ever, the calm on her face was so intense that I didn't want to wake her up, I kissed her on the forehead and quietly snuck out of the bed and went up to draw the curtains, a pleasant beam of morning light fell upon the room. I turned around to see if I had disturbed her sleep, her body was glistening in the morning sun. The glaze of the morning sun on her flawless skin made her look like an angel; but the light seemed to have disturbed her sleep, she squeaked like a mice rubbing her eyes with her palm, there was a smile on her face and watching her smile was the best thing that could have happened to me that day.'Sone do na please...' she said it in a such an innocent voice that I did not have the heart to do anything against her wish. I drew the curtain back and snuck under the blanket. Her skin touched mine, badan me current daud gaya aisa laga. It was the most wonderful feeling that I had ever experienced. I was ecstatic, but at the same time a strange feeling gripped me, the fear of losing her. Things seemed to be too rosy to be real. What if things didn't workout, what if she started hating me. These thoughts gave me a chill, phir maine socha jo hua nahi hai uske baare me soch ke faida nahi hai. It may happen that things turn out really well for us, we may stay together for eternity, kuchh bhi ho sakta hai."

"Ye sahi baat bola hai tune, isi baat pe ke sutta ho jaae" Drunk Shantanu sounded really different.

We lit a cigarette each and lied down letting the smoke in. I let the silence of the night get into me, my eyes were feeling the weight of sleep, I took a couple of aggressive puffs to shake it off and then continued.

"We spent the entire weekened togehter, full of masti and enjoyment, life seemed to be perfect and just like that the time to bid good bye came."

"Phir kab miloge?" Poorvi asked, innocently.

"December me during the vacations, in about three months."

"Three month... it's a long time away." She sounded disappointed.

"Ya... it is" I was packing my stuff and was just listening but not understanding what she was saying.

"Good then!!!" She yelled and stormed out of the room banging the door behind her.

"Bhai mai zyada relation me to nahi raha hu magar itna to jaanta hu ki jab girl friend baat kar rahi ho to listen to her, always listen to her" Shantanu was giving me some of his 'GYAAN'

"I realized I had hurt her, I went after her and held her in my arms. Her eyes were red and swollen, she had been sobbing.

I felt sad and angry at the same time, sad for the look at her face and angry because I could not sense her anguish and my actions had made her shed those valuable tears. 'I'm really sorry Poorvi, please... come on...' 'chhodo jaane do, baat nahi karni hai mujhe tumse...' she pushed me away, I leaned into her, wrapped my arms around her neck from behind and planted a kiss on her neck. 'Dont start here...' 'To andar chalo' I said cheekily.

I somehow persuaded her to come back to the room.

"Poorvi jab tum bologi mai aaunga be assured, iske liye tum ro rahi thi... hadd hai, chalo muskurao... ye aasu ke saath tumhara look bigad jaata hai, jaate jaate please don't cry."

"Phir kya tha smile kiya usne, it was the perfect look, try to picturize it and you'll understand what I'm trying to say."

"I can't promise how well I can picturize her right now my senses are compromised, you know that don't you? "

"Her smile was forcing its way through her sullen face, it was like a ray of light forcing its way through the dark clouds, it drew a perfect picture when her smile reached her eyes, this smile made her already beautiful eyes look even more beautiful, her relentless sobbing had made her face turn red, pale red, this pale red brushed across her perfectly fair complexion, her marble smooth skin, her red eyes, red nose, moist under eyes and a slight snort under her nose made her look so very innocent. You'll just have to picture her believe me there are no words that can perfectly describe her. Gradually the smile broke into a laughter it felt as if the sun was beaming down in the room, she swept the stray hairs off her face and jokingly punched me. I can still feel the love, the affection and the trust that was packed in that punch."

'So when are you leaving?'

'Actually, I'll have to leave now. The flight is in 2 hours.'

'I'll wash my face and be back.'

'You're coming to the airport?'

'Obviously, what kind of a question is this?'

'I just thought... kuchh nahi, chalo taiyaar ho jaao, mai apne room me hu,' I knew it wasn't possible to talk her out of this. After 5 minutes or so, she came and walked straight into my room. She was looking stunning; the session of sobbing had left the portion under her eyes swollen, along with a definite captivating sparkle in them that could have hypnotized anyone. Every inch of her body was fabulous, and the fact that today I would have to say goodbye to her was killing me.' Normally I am not the emotional kind, but today I had to summon all my energy to hold myself together. It was painful, very painful.

'That's it then, chalo...' The pain in her voice was evident from the way she said those words. I was sad, really sad, but there wasn't anything I could have done to reduce the pain that was crippling both me and her.

'Ya, the cab has arrived, we should leave.' I looked at her; she was still looking sad. When the cab started, the philosophical side of me sprang up to explain an analogy between life and a car to Poorvi. 'See Poorvi, while we set off on a journey, we fill the tank with fuel, much like how we fill our hearts with hopes and excitement. As the journey progresses, the level of fuel comes down, and by the time the journey is over, the tank is nearly empty. Similarly, at the end of something nice and wonderful, all the excitement generally turns into sadness. But just like we refill the tank after it has gone empty, we should do the same. This journey of ours is over, the metaphorical tank has gone empty now, but does this mean that the journey is over? No, we'll refill, and refill real soon.'

'That is good and also quite an unusual observation. Nonetheless, I got your point, and we should look forward to our next rendezvous and hope it is as awesome as this was. Thanks for coming; I understand it must have been difficult for you, bunking classes and all,' Poorvi said. She wasn't fully cheerful but sounded positive nonetheless.

'Pagal hai kya? Where is the difficulty in bunking? Plus, I got to meet you, and missing classes for this is a small price. Believe me, I can do this over and over again; only you need to be free. Mai to kabhi bhi aa jaunga.'

'Theek hai, theek hai, chalo ab jao, flight ka boarding start ho gaya, itna senti dialogues mat maaro.'

'Theek hai, chalo, bye, phir milenge.' I kissed her on the forehead and said goodbye. As I headed for the final security check, I turned to see her for one last time. She was there, wiping a tear off her cheek. She waved at me and faked a smile, as if saying 'don't worry about me, I'll be fine, you go...' I did not want to leave, but again, we don't always get what we want. If we did, that would make this world perfect, wouldn't it?

"That's quite a story. It's hard to believe, considering the things that had happened between you two. Sahi hai be senapati. I am not able to understand one thing though; things were so good between you two, at least it seemed that way from your narrative. How did you screw it up?" Shantanu assumed that the break-up was my fault, and it was my fault alright, but I just didn't like people jumping to conclusions. The fact that he concluded it even after downing 4 bottles of beer made me think whether it would be obvious to others as well.

"Saale tu kaise assume kar raha hai ki galti meri thi?" I countered.

"Chal tu hi bata de thi ya nahi?"

"Ha, meri hi thi, magar saale, assume mat kar be, behenchod, ganda lagta hai." Shantanu started laughing.

"Chal batata hu, but I'll need another cigarette, shayad tujhe bhi chahiye, you look sleepy." We lit another cigarette.

"Abe saale, college me tune ye kabhi mention kyu nahi kiya tha? All we knew was that you were after some girl in Gangtok, aur wo bhi tere ko theek-thaak type bhaau de rahi hai." Shantanu was surprised that I had not mentioned Poorvi despite the 'achievement' that it was in its own rights.

"Abe Rinku ko maine ye bataya tha, and he had promised to be discreet about it. Kisiko lagta nahi tha ki meri bhi girlfriend ho sakti hai. Plus, koi mere pe shak bhi nahi karta tha because I did not spend hours talking to her on the phone every day." I explained.

"Let me guess, your uncommunicative nature was one of the reasons for your fall out?" He made another guess.

"Yes, this was one of the reasons, magar ek baat sun ab agar ek baar bhi aise guess kiya to I'll make sure you regret it." This guessing game was getting onto my nerves.

"Things were great between us; however, at some level, I was always skeptical about how smooth our relationship was. We never had any fights or arguments. The closest we came to an argument was a debate, 'School life or college life, which is better,' and that too after 20 minutes of discussion we settled on a common conclusion. Things were too chocolaty between us, and that made me doubt the very reality of our relationship. This chocolaty phase continued for more than a year, actually not just a year, it went well into the second year of our relationship."

"Sahi to hai be, what was wrong with that? Koi ladai nahi hua to kya hua?" Shantanu was unable to understand the logic.

"I'll draw a parallel; probably you'll see it then. See, if you do not catch a cold for say 2-3 years, what does that imply? It means that you are at a greater risk of getting affected by jaundice. I did not mind the occasional cold in our relationship; what I dreaded was the jaundice. I was just hoping that it was not the lull before a storm."

"So how did it turn into a 'jaundice'?"

Chapter 5

THE BREAK UP

"See, there are only a finite number of topics in this world that you can talk about. And generally, you exhaust these within the first 6 months of the relationship, and then the relationship is carried forward by fights, arguments, and quarrels. You see we did not have any quarrels, so after some time, we had exhausted the topics that we could talk about. Our already small conversations started getting shorter by the day. It eventually reached a stage where we would simply ask about each other's well-being, stay quiet for some time, and then customarily ask 'Kuchh eventful hua kya aaj' before hanging up."

"Abe mujhe bhi samajh nahi aata hai ki ye couples kya baat karte hai itne der tak." Shantanu again agreed with me.

"Exactly, this was one of the reasons why she eventually broke it off with me."

"What were the other reasons?" Shantanu asked.

"See since we never had any conflicts, I kind of let my guards down."

"Guards down matlab?"

"See when you have a nagging girlfriend, you are a bit careful in your choice of words. You never know kab kya aake tujhe pichhwade me kaat daalega. In my case, things were different; we never had any differences, and she wasn't 'nagging' either, so after a few initial months, I did not think much before saying anything. Little did I know that these things would combine together to have effects of catastrophic proportions."

"Abe ye to hai be, while in a relationship you should be meticulous in your choice of words. But I understand your situation, you did not realize the potential danger that was hovering over you. So tell me to what extent did you let your 'guard down'?" he asked.

"Things were not very passionate between us at that time, and I regret it now but I had started taking her for granted. The big fallout happened on the night of our seniors' job party. Hum log masti se daaru pi rahe the, we were enjoying the most joyous moment of our seniors. Sabhi saare inhibitions bhool ke carefree tareeke se pee rahe the, ek dusre ka maazaak uda rahe the in short hostel life enjoy kar rahe the to the fullest. I was busy gathering 'fundes' from 'Mangal Bhaiya,' you remember him, right?"

"Ha be of course I remember him."

"He was pouring his wisdom on me, all the tricks that were needed to survive electrical engineering, the tricks on how to crack the interviews, how to sidetrack the interviewer if you are not sure about the answers. At the same moment Poorvi ka call aaya, I disconnected it, she called again, I disconnected again, and again and again... I didn't talk to her because I knew it's never good to talk to a girl when you're drunk."

"This was a good thing that you did. But sensing by your tone, she did not take it all that well."

"Abe how 'unwell' she took it was evident from the text that she eventually sent."

"Kya likha usne... Teri to lag gayi hogi pakka."

"Kuchh zyada nahi, just... 'Call me NOW!!!' it sure was just a three-word text, but its implications were huge. I felt mighty offended by her showing authority, rather stamping authority. I was too drunk to think rationally. Had I not been inebriated I would have certainly acted differently. In my fit of rage, I called her:

'Mera calls kyu disconnect kar rahe ho?' Poorvi asked point-blank.

'Dekh Poorvi, abhi hostel me party ho rahi hai, this is not a good time to talk, plus I've had a bit too much to drink.'

'Nahi Ajit aajkal tum mujhe bahut ignore kar rahe ho. It's way after midnight, you should not be drinking anymore. Ab jaake chup chaap so jaao, we'll talk tomorrow.'

I was already upset, and her last statement pushed me over the edge. I started yelling at her, reminding her repeatedly that it was my life and I didn't need to be taught how to live.

'This is exactly what I meant, Ajit, drinking makes you a beast, you are yelling at me in front of all your friends.

I liked you because you were sensitive to my emotions, but thanks for proving me wrong. Call me when you are sober.' and she hung up..." Recollecting the altercation made me really, really sad...

"Tu tension mat le re, teri koi galti nahi thi... Yes, maybe you lost your cool and had that outburst which you could have avoided, but again, you were drunk, so..." Shantanu was taking my side on this, but it hardly made any difference. The sense of losing her came rushing back. If only I had handled that situation differently, things could have been different between us. I might not have been alone right now, talking about her to a friend. I realized alcohol makes you a different person altogether, a bad one at that too. After that incident, I had restricted my alcohol intake to just beers, but I guess it was a bit too late.

"Abe ab royega kya. Jo hona tha wo ho gaya, ab tension mat le," Shantanu tried to pep me up, but it didn't help me much.

"Before that night, I used to wonder why we never had any fights, and now that we had this fight, I wish we had never fought. That was the beginning of the downslide in our relationship. However hard we tried to get over it, we just couldn't. Things that would otherwise have gone by as non-events now led to our frequent fights; it had reached a point where we had started annoying each other, and then the inevitable happened."

"Kya hua? Matlab what was the final blow?"

"Abe if I don't fill you in regarding the build-up to the final showdown, you may not be able to fully relate to our situation." Shantanu was curious to know the main cause of our split, but jumping directly to it wouldn't have done justice to either him or the story.

"Chal theek hai, bring on the buildup, but sasuri ek sutta break please."

"Abe please kyu bol raha hai, ek ek maarte hai magar saale kitna phukega." Though I was a smoker, I was not a heavy one. Normally I had 3 or at max 4 ciggs per week. But this wasn't a normal day, night out with a college buddy talking about my ex-flame, this by no means was a 'normal day.' I mean how often are you able to have a night out with your college friend, especially after 2 years of passing out. It was a renaissance of sorts. We lit a fag each and silently took puffs. Shantanu held the cigarette high, looking at the tip he said...

"Abe ek philosophical baat mujhe bhi strike kar rahi hai, see this cigarette is like your relationship, your first fight is similar to lighting the cig. You put out the matchstick but it left your cig burning. Each puff was like a small fight, inconsequential otherwise, but since the cig is lit, it was eating up your relationship. Had you somehow averted the situation of lighting it, things could have been different, but once lit, there is no stopping it, it's just a matter of time before the entire cig is used up depending upon the frequency and strength of each puff..."

"Ultimate be kela... bahut philosophical baatein kar raha hai matlab daru kaam kar raha hai." We had a long laugh at my last comment. It wasn't particularly funny, but don't know why we found it hilarious.

"Chal ab tell me about the metaphorical puffs that you took."

"After the first outburst, we decided to look beyond the differences and start afresh. But to be honest, that episode had left a big void in our relationship. A gap had been created that unfortunately neither made an effort to bridge. Our relationship hit a new low when I visited her 'Facebook' page. She had recently uploaded pictures from her trip to Nathula. I had no idea that she had gone for a trip; this wouldn't have been a problem before our big fight. We trusted each other, but now it was an issue, a big one. What made me upset was the fact that now we had reached a point where we thought sharing our plans with each other was not important. I was going through her pictures, thinking how things have gone sour between us, when I saw a group picture of her. She was resting her head on a guy's shoulder. I couldn't believe my eyes. Agreed we were not having the best of times as a couple, but I wasn't prepared for this. My heart started knocking against my ribs; I started sweating and feeling restless. My body was reacting in an odd way. I thought I might collapse."

"Phek mat saale, koi photo dekh ke kaise faint ho sakta hai..." Shantanu abruptly broke my flow, that too with such a wild remark. He was acting weird. One moment he was all philosophical and sensitive, and in moments like this, he was blunt and insensitive.

"Sahi chutiya hai be tu, behenchod saale. I was in love with this girl for the last 7 years; to see her getting comfortable with someone else destroyed me. True, things were a bit bumpy, but I had not expected this from her.

Sach bolu to there was a little corner in my heart that was saying that there was an explanation for all this. But at that time I was blinded by my anger and jealousy. I did not allow myself to see beyond those pictures. All that I saw was my girlfriend getting comfortable with someone else."

"Yaar, I know at times like those you can't force yourself to see past the things that are there on the face. You should have waited to listen to her side of the story, but again when you are in love, it's difficult to use logic to arrive at conclusions. I'm already having a bad feeling about this, but tell me what did you do next?"

"I don't know if I should have done this or not, but I went through the rest of her pictures, and I wasn't surprised seeing what I saw. There were multiple photographs where she was with the same guy, just the two of them. It occurred to me that she wanted me to see those photographs; she wanted to indicate that she has had enough of me. Why else would she have uploaded those pictures on the most popular networking site? Was she looking to break it off with me? Was she going to end the relationship? These thoughts brought a silent tear that rolled down my cheek. I had not cried even during the worst phase of ragging. You know I was tough, really tough. But she made me weep; she was the special one whose loss I could not bear. The single tear that rolled out opened the flood gates. I locked myself in the room and cried. I cried long, thinking that this would take some load off my heart. Well, it didn't; instead, it made me angrier. I wanted to confront her. If she wanted to end it off, she should do it to my face; she had no right to torture me this way. I picked my phone to call her, but something stopped me. I don't know why, but I decided not to call her. I wanted to give her an opportunity to explain herself and come clean about the entire episode."

"Ye sahi kiya be, there's always two aspects to a story. You should never conclude something without hearing both sides." Shantanu explained.

"What you are saying is true, but there was just one problem though, I did call her that day." I replied.

"Jaanta tha mai, koi aashiq itna samajhdaar nahi hota hai. Kab call kiya?" Shantanu asked.

"Uss waqt to maine call nahi kiya, magar the pain was killing me. The thought of her being with someone else drove me crazy. I was dying to confront her, but fearing that I might ruin something beyond repair, I refrained myself from calling her. But the shattered lover inside me wanted something that could reduce the pain I felt inside."

"Abe bol na I wanted daaru..."

"Ha, I wanted daaru, and I did just that. Gaya daaru ke adde pe jaake ek full bottle rum ka leke aa gaya. Room ka darwaaza band kiya, lights off kiya, laptop pe gaane lagaya, aur pyaar se peg banane laga. I thought alcohol would help me forget her, but instead, it made my pain worse. The song running in the background made matters worse for me. All those songs made me miss her; there were either memories associated with those songs, or I ended up picturizing us in those songs. After another couple of pegs, I could not take it anymore. The alcohol that I was pumping into my system reacted with the already present rage. It is a known fact that alcohol destroys your brain cells. Little did I know that it can affect you immediately; it can impair your decision-making ability. I found it the hard way. Though I had decided to give her an opportunity to explain and not confront her, I couldn't fight my inner instinct, the instinct of a wounded lover."

"Saale funde mat de, bata call kar ke kya bola?" Shantanu got irritated with the detailed explanation.

"Theek hai re bhai point pe aata hu, gussa kyu ho raha hai sasuri... I let drunken Ajit take over my actions, I reached for my phone. I was so drunk that I could not even press the keys properly. After some effort, I managed to dial her. It was 2:30 in the morning, way too late to call anybody, let alone girls, to that add the fact that I was far from sober."

"Saale kya bola ye to bata baar baar tu explanation dene me chala jaata hai. Kya chutiyapa hai be behenchod." Shantanu was visibly irritated by my constant description of how wrong was the thing that I did.

"Call lagagya maine, she received it and she responded with a voice that was soaked deep in sleep.

'Hellllooooo... Bahut late ho gaya hai, subah baat karte hai na pllllleeeease....' The way she extended the lleeee in please made my heart go soft, all the anger nearly evaporated off but at the same time the pictures of her with that boy flashed before my eyes and all the anger came rushing back, the feeling was so intense that I was blinded by it, I yelled back at her with all the capacity I had in my lungs.

'Tu samajhti kya hai jab mann karega tabhi baat karegi... Abhi mujhe baat karni hai aur tujhe sunna padega'

'Kya baat hai Ajit, itna gussa kyu kar rahe ho' she nearly cried." Recalling that I had woken her up in the middle of night and then yelled at her that made her cry.

I felt aweful all over again, I had once promised that I would always keep her happy and in contrary I had made her cry, a drop of tear rolled down from my eyes, I was genuinely sad for the happenings of that day. I covered my face with my palm and used my thumb to wipe off the tear from the corner of my eye. Seeing me shantanu came over to my side and patted on my shoulder, I needed much more than just a pat but this was all I was getting.

"Abe ab kya karega, jo hona tha wo ho gaya na, you shouldn't have called her but again sometimes things that we never want to happen happens. I am not supporting what you did but 9 out of 10 guys would have acted similarly. Don't be so hard on yourself".

He meant well but it didn't make me feel any better. I didn't want to continue telling the story of how I managed to make the girl who loved me so much hate me instead. But then I had to finish telling it, it wouldn't have been fair on Shantanu to be left hanging. So I continued.

"Abe theek hai koi nahi, sun aagey ki story maine kaise apni marwaayi.

'Poorvi... Ye bata wo Natuhula waala banda kaun tha...' I shot this at her blankly, almost coldly. She wasn't expecting this to come up at this point in time.

'Kaun ladka, kya keh rahe ho Ajit?' She was rattled by the question, to say the least.

'Zyaada bholi mat ban tu, tune wo pictures jaan bujh ke upload kiya na so that I see it. You want to break it off, don't you? Well, you should have the heart to do it to my face, directly bol deti, ab mai tumse bore ho gayi hu so bye, itna naatak kyu karna?' I was shouting on top of my voice; I did not give her any chance to explain. She was astounded by my allegation; of course, now I know it was an allegation, but back then, I thought that was the ultimate truth.

'Ajit tum nashe me ho, please go to sleep, tomorrow we shall talk about whatever you want to talk. I'll explain everything, but please Ajit abhi tum so jaao.' She was literally begging me to let go of this for now, but stupidity had struck me to such a level that I couldn't sense the genuine concern in her voice. I was blinded by the preconceived notion that she was cheating on me.

'Achchha so that you have time to think of an excuse, just answer my questions. I know you can manipulate me when I am sober, so just tell me who the hell was that guy.'

'Wo mera cousin hai Ajit... Don't think too much, just go and sleep.' She was getting annoyed now.

'Nahi sona hai mujhe, you have lost the right to command me. Mai wahi karunga jo mera mann hoga. Make peace with that lady.'

'Tu phone rakh Ajit, I can't take your nonsense anymore. I am not your slave that you'll call me at any time of the night and start yelling. Don't you dare cross your limit and violate my dignity.' She had grown really-really angry. I should have stopped my foolishness and apologized instead I continued the argument.

'Tu mere pe chilla rahi hai Poorvi, ulta chor kotwaal ko daante... Ek to khud kisi dusre ladke ke saath masti kar rahi hai aur mere pe gussa dikha rahi hai.'

'Tu chup reh gadhe, kuchh bhi bole jaa raha hai tu, akal naam ki koi cheez hai tujhme. Tab se call karke bhauke jaa raha hai, jaat dikha diya ne tune apna. Mai bol rahi hu ki wo mera cousin tha to tere ko samajh nahi aa raha hai kya. But I think a swine like you has no sense of family.' She was very angry; she had never ever been offensive before, the pitch in which she said those words showed exactly how angry she was. But stupidity had struck me with all its force; I was in no mood to stop. I retaliated and retaliated in a manner which I regret till date. The words that I used were so offensive that I can't even tell you what I had said. I wish I was dead before I let those words out of my mouth. The remarks that I had made about her would demean the entire humanity." I could not believe that I had actually made those filthy remarks about her.

"'Dikha hi diya na tune apni aukaad. Yahi kehna reh gaya tha.' She was sobbing, or rather crying; it was then I realized what I had done. I had ruined the relationship beyond repair. Before I could apologize, she added, 'You have crossed the line, Ajit; I had never thought that I would hear those words ever in my life, and that too from you. I can't believe that I ever thought of spending the rest of my life with a moron like you. Thanks, Ajit, for stopping me from making the biggest blunder of my life. I'll always remember you... good bye...' and she hung up. I knew things were over; I had bent the relationship to such a level that it could not be repaired. A cold sweat descended on my forehead, and I collapsed, only to wake up the next morning."

"Sorry, man, for making you remember such a horrible event," Shantanu was sympathetic about my tragedy.

"I woke up the next morning; the hangover had left a terrible headache. I could not fully recall the events that had transpired the previous night. My head was killing me; I looked around to find my phone. It was lying on the floor next to the empty bottle of rum; it then struck me that I drank the entire bottle all by myself. With a bad feeling, I reached for my phone; it had one message from Poorvi. I had a hazy recollection of last night. I had called her, we had a fight, what did we fight about, was it about the photographs, how bad did we fight? How did it end? To what extent I had accused her? All these questions started swirling in my head, and I started getting a really bad feeling about all this. More often than not I screw up whenever I talk to someone when I am drunk. Fearing the worst, I opened the message, it read... 'I am not angry, Ajit, but remember one thing, only cheap guys call girls when they are drunk... It may help you in your future relationships.' Suddenly all the things that had happened last night came flashing before my eyes. The argument, the yelling, the crying, everything came flashing. I finally recalled the last words Poorvi had said; it's then that I realized we had broken up. I hoped it was a dream, I silently prayed for it to not be true. However, I knew that the worst had happened; I had insulted Poorvi, yelled at her, and even made her cry. I recollected the entire conversation word by word. Her last words were 'You have crossed the line, Ajit; I had never thought that I would hear those words ever in my life, and that too from you. I can't believe that I ever thought of spending the rest of my life with a moron like you. Thanks, Ajit, for stopping me from making the biggest blunder of my life. I'll always remember you... good bye'." I was already gloomy, and recalling the final showdown did not help me at all. I sunk deep in remorse. Shantanu patted me on my back; even he felt sad, sad for me, sad for my loss, and probably sad for my foolishness. I waited for a couple of seconds and continued describing my pain.

"I had done something that could not be retracted. However, I had to apologize to her. She definitely would not have taken me back, but she surely deserved an apology."

"That was really intelligent on your part. You did hurt her, whether you were sober or not at that time was a totally different issue."

"I called her up; she did not respond. I tried many times, still no reply, but I would not give up. Eventually, she took my call. 'I am really sorry, Poorvi, bilkul hosh me nahi tha. I did not mean what I had said. Please give me another chance,' I was literally begging.

'Nahi Ajit, things are over between us.' She was really angry.

'Please, Poorvi, I'll change...' I nearly broke down.

'You know something, when people are drunk they speak what's there in their heart, all those things that you said were there within you, you may not have said it if you were sober, but you had that suspicion about me and my commitment towards you. Last night will repeat itself every time you drink, I can't take that risk again, Ajit.'

'I'll quit drinking, mai badal jaunga, Poorvi, tum jaisa kahogi mai waisa ban jaunga. Bas mujhe ek chance aur de do please. I have loved you since childhood; I still love you and will always love you... Please ek aakhri baar maaf karde yaar, aagey se kabhi kuchh galat nahi karunga...' I was crying.

'Nahi Ajit, I'm sorry but I am not ready to take that chance,' she was also hurting, she did not want to let me go, but she also was not willing to forgive me for what I had done the other night. She was sure that she did not want to give me another chance.

'Poorvi Please....' my voice was now beginning to choke. I had not cried that way ever in my life; I was begging her to forgive me, but she was not willing to flinch, she was determined.

'I had always believed that you were a good guy; I never imagined that you would stoop so low...' I was tired of all the begging and crying; I wiped the tear off my face and asked. 'Meri ek galti ke wajah se saara blame mujhpe aa gaya na... Wo photo wala banda to pura out of focus hi chala gaya na?' I was angry because even after requesting so much she was not willing to take a step backward.

"This is exactly what I mean, Ajit; you can't change, not today, not tomorrow, never... You just can't change..."

"Oh great... If you've decided, then go enjoy with your 'cousin.' I have begged enough."

"Don't you dare go there again, Ajit. We are done here. I don't want to hear from you ever again," and she disconnected.

"I'm sorry, man..." Shantanu patted me on my back. He knew I was howling inside; that was the worst thing that

I had ever experienced, and talking about it saddened me beyond comprehension.

"I tried to get in touch with her after that day, but with no luck. She had changed her number, unfriended me on all the social networking sites. In short, she had severed all the threads that connected us."

"Abe, back in college, nobody had the slightest idea that you had gone through so much. You never wore that typical 'devdas' look."

"I always pretended that I was fine. But I was dying inside. The fact that I held it in within me made me suffer all the more. When I could not take it anymore, I decided to go see her. I went to her college and I went directly to her hostel. Waha gate pe ek guard tha.

'Bhaiya, Poorvi ko bula dijiye na,' I requested the guard.

'Aap kaun hai? Poorvi kaun hai aapka?' The guard said in an interrogative tone.

'Arre bandhu, aap boliye Poorvi ko 'Namesh Khirodkar' aaya hai, cousin hu mai uska...'

'Theek hai, aap waiting room me baithiye, mai bulata hu,' and he left. After 5 mins or so, I saw Poorvi walk down the stairs; she was looking astonishing. Now that she had made it clear that she was not available for me, it made her all the more desirable. As she approached the waiting room, my nervousness grew. Would she even talk to me? How would she react to me using a fake name to get her out of her room? I was busy juggling all these questions when she came inside. I stood up to greet her, wearing a nervous smile.

'What the hell are you doing here?' This was the last expression I had expected. I had traveled all the way from my college, and this was her reaction. Anyway, I did not want to end up having a fight this time around. So I politely replied to her,

'Arre, tumse milne aaya hu, kaisi ho?' I tried to sound casual.

'Mai bahut achchhi hu, pata chal gaya na ab jaao yaha se.' She had not cooled off even a bit.

'Aisa na kar Poorvi, itne dur se tere se milne aaya hu. Sun to le, kya kehna chahta hu.'

'Tu bolna chahta hai? Theek hai bol, aur jab bolna khatam ho jaae, to nikal jaana samjha.' I had had enough of her. I did try to apologize, but she would not allow me to. Mai bhi irritate ho chuka tha, aur socha bahut ho gaya. There was no point in getting your self-respect beaten down.

'Actually Poorvi, ek word kehna hai mujhe... 'BYE," and I stormed out of the room. I didn't even look back to see how she reacted. However painful it was for me, I decided to close that chapter forever. At least I would not initiate reconciliation again."

"Abe, sahi kiya be. It was logical to give a last shot at trying to salvage something that was eternal to your very survival. It didn't go as you had expected, but again it was not in your control..."

"So that was how I met Poorvi, made her fall in love with me, stayed together for 3 years, and then split. But I think there is one final twist that awaits me," I said smiling cheekily.

"Abe, ha be, saale itna senti kar diya tune ki mai to bhool hi gaya ki Poorvi ka message aaya tha aaj. Kya baat kiya? Kaise number mila usko tera. There was a spark in his eyes; it felt really good to see that someone was genuinely concerned about my feelings.

"Abe kuchh khaas nahi. Both of us avoided talking about our last confrontation. Apart from that awkwardness, everything else was great. I think this time it might work out between us," I was really hopeful about things working out this time around.

"Aur ha, number kaha se mila usko, that's a mystery. Usne nahi bataya, but I don't care how she got it as long as she had it. Still, there is one loose end. What happened today that had not happened in the last 2 years that made her call me? Sasuri, ye baat samajh me nahi aa rahi hai." I smiled out.

"Yes, that is one thing that confuses me, magar don't bring this up with her immediately. She may not like it. Once things turn out to be the way it was earlier, then you can playfully ask. But not now, enjoy the attention that you are getting."

"Ha be, sahi bol raha hai. I'll try not to screw it up this time around, even if it means not knowing certain things."

"Sahi be saale, masti aa gaya tera love story sun ke. Baal suraj bhi nikal gaya, rook mai coffee banata hu, mujhe office ke liye nikalna hai, tu bhi packing shuru kar de aur udd ja." Shantanu was preparing to freshen up.

"It was great opening up to you, man. Sasuri yaha bahut akela feel kar raha tha, really glad you came." We took the coffee with a cigarette, freshened up, and went our ways.

Chapter 6

FLYING TO BANGALORE

"Bhaiya, volume kum kijiye..." I was having one of the worst hangovers; my head was exploding, and the high volume of the 'bhojpuri item song' playing in the cab wasn't helping.

"Late-night party hua tha sir?" The cab driver, Abdul, inquired, reducing the volume. I didn't reply; I sat there in the cab, using the window to support my exploding head. I was in no position to talk; I was too hungover to either listen to or make any kind of noise.

As the cab hustled its way through the dusty traffic of 'Andheri,' I lay there reminiscing the happenings of last night. It was one of the most wonderful times that I had spent in years. Getting to talk to a college friend after a gap of over two years was in itself rewarding, and that too when you've stayed the entire night discussing your lost love was all the more satisfying. There are times when you need to have a confidant, someone whom you could trust with your secrets howsoever shady it might be. Mine was not shady by any means, but still, you can't go about telling everyone about your failed love story. I felt good talking about Poorvi, talking about the good and the bad times that I had with her. I had not expected that it would be so relieving to talk about the past with someone.

"Sir earphone hai kya? Wo kya hai ki bina kuchh sune gaadi chalane me thodi dikkat hoti hai," he added with a sheepish grin.

I reached for my bag, took the earphone out, and handed it to him without saying a word.

"Sir lagta hai bahut ganda hangover hai aapko, kahi neembu paani ke liye roku?"

"Nahi Abdul, pehle hi late ho rakha hai, aap gaadi chalaiye..." I was already getting late; I couldn't afford a detour. I popped an aspirin instead. 'Poorvi's message' my phone beeped, sounding the customized message tone that I had made yesterday. I had this habit of customizing things to suit me.

'GM, have a safe flight,' it read.

'Thanks...' I replied; I was so hungover that I did not want to continue the conversation.

'Kya hua? Not feeling well?'

'Ha thoda headache ho raha hai...' I knew how the message would have sounded to her; I was not putting any effort into continuing the chat. All I wanted to do was to lay motionless and let the alcohol settle down. There is nothing worse than a bad hangover; it literally (figuratively) kills you.

One good thing about a 'REPAIRED' relationship is that you are allowed a few goof-ups without inviting serious consequences. Had I exhibited this kind of behavior when we were a couple, I would have been at the receiving end of her pleasantries, but not now. Instead, she texted back:

'Kyu? aisa kya kiya tha kal ;)' She was being cheeky. I did not want to lie to her, but again, I did not know how she would respond if I told her that I was up all night drinking with a college buddy. It might bring back memories that she may not like to recall. But again, there was one question that was not clear, what made her change her mind? The last time I saw her, she was so mad that she did not even want to talk to me. What happened after that that made her forget all my wrongdoings? I was trapped in the maze of these questions trying to find my way out when my phone beeped again:

'?'

I realized that I had not replied to her, and she was growing impatient...

'Arre kuchh nahi, thoda kaam zyaada tha office me, packing and stuff.' We guys know that packing is not an issue at all, but you can use this excuse with inexplicable effect on women.

'Ok, you may want to take some rest now, call me once you reach Bangalore or whenever you feel like talking... Happy journey, TC, bye.'

'Sure, I definitely will... Bye.' I did not want her to interpret that I was trying to avoid her. I wasn't avoiding her; it was just that I wasn't feeling all that great and wasn't putting much thought into the words that I was typing.

I thought that the texting would stop, and I'd get some rest, and I had just leaned against the window when the phone beeped again:

'One last text, I LOVE YOU,' it read; this was the last thing that I was expecting. My headache was gone; what on earth was going on with her.

First, she contacts me after a gap of nearly two years, and now when we were just warming up our relationship, she says 'I love you,' and that too completely out of the blue, out of the context, and to put it in a broader sense, out of nowhere. I knew even if I tore my hair out (though there isn't much left) I couldn't find an answer to this. I was confused, to say the least. True, I was still in love with her; my passion for her had not diminished even a bit. I loved her just the way I had loved her earlier, but even this could not clear the doubt that had eclipsed my mind. Why did she re-establish contact with me? What I remember was that the last time she sounded pretty sure that she did not want to hear my voice, ever. What was it that made her change her mind and change it to this extent? She was not just back to talking terms with me; she was being open about her feelings, about her re-discovered love.

Something did not add up; this was not consistent with her. I had never expected that she would try to establish contact with me, and that she would say 'I LOVE YOU' wasn't what I had imagined. I was wrestling with these thoughts in my mind when she texted again:

'SORRY, I know you were not expecting this, but I mean every syllable of it, I truly LOVE you, and I do not regret it.'

What was going on with her today? First, what was with her saying 'I LOVE YOU,' and then saying 'I do not regret it'? Was she thinking that I was expecting her to regret those words?

I was not sure what had gotten into her; was she high or something? Or had the stars aligned themselves in such a way that it was conspiring to make my love story a success? The lines from the popular Bollywood movie Om Shanti Om inspired by the book 'The Alchemist' started working in my head.

'Agar kisi ko puri shiddat se chaho to saari kaaynaat usko tumse milane ki saajish me jut jaati hai.'

I still had to reply to her; I texted back, trying my best to mellow down the emotion from it:

'Don't be sorry; in fact, even I am not totally over you.' I hit the send button. I now started to think of the possible interpretations that this sentence might have.

When I typed it, I wanted it to mean that no doubt I love you, but I can still survive without you. It was important that I approached this sensibly to have the desirable result, as this was the person of my dreams that I was dealing with. It had been long since we had last seen each other; even back then, things did not end the way we would have liked it to end.

This might be my only chance to somehow try and salvage an otherwise dead and drowning relationship. And the fact that the possibility of this actually happening was very high, considering that the renewal of our relationship was actually initiated by Poorvi, made my steps all the more important and consequential.

'I'm glad :)' Poorvi replied. I did not know how to respond to this.

I wasn't in a place where I could've stressed my mind and come up with something intelligent, so I decided not to reply; after all, it wasn't a question.

'Dawai li?' she texted again. My actions could not be explained; on any other occasion, I would have been over the moon at the attention that was being showered upon me by her. But on the contrary, I was getting irritated by her repeated and never-ending queries.

"Ya le li hai, actually got to go security clearance ke liye late ho raha hu, call you once I reach Bangalore, tc bye..."

"Bye, have a safe journey..." I was kind of relieved that the conversation was over.

I was praying for my headache to subside before I boarded the flight. I've had my share of hungover flights, and believe me, it's not pleasing at all. If there was anything to learn from those experiences, it was to never board flights until the alcohol in your body has settled down. The driver's snub remark interrupted my benediction:

"Good morning, sirji.... ab baaki ki neend flight me poora kijiyega..." He added it with a broad smile, thinking I would be amused by his sense of humour... Well, I wasn't...

"Chal bill de..." I am seldom disrespectful to anyone, but his misplaced humour did not go too well with me.

"Theek hai, sir... ye lijiye." He handed me the bill along with a Saridon, I was surprised...

"Ye kya de rahe ho?"

"Sir, le lijiye Saridon, theek ho jaega... udne se pehle le lijiyega..."

"Magar ye..." I was lost for words.

"Arre sir, bil ke saath goli free." After my response to his last comment, the last thing I was expecting was another gag.

"Dhanyavaad, bandhu..." I was thoroughly impressed by his humanity. The fact that I had not been all that kind to him during the entire journey made his kindness even more remarkable.

After settling the bill, I headed towards the terminal. There, I was supposed to meet Anjali and Nisha. Because of the awful hangover, I had completely forgotten about them. Just as I was about to reach the terminal, I saw a lemonade stall just outside the main gate. I took my phone out to check the time. There was another hour and a half before the scheduled takeoff, which meant I had at least half an hour to spare.

"Should I call Nisha to find out where they are?" I thought out loud. I decided against it; lemonade was something that was higher on my priority list at that moment.

I looked towards the stall again; it seemed to be calling out to me. I heeded its call and walked straight towards it. There was a big clay pot covered with a wet red cloth. The quality of water was definitely suspicious, but at that time, the supposedly compromised water was the least of my concerns. The brim of the pot was decorated with fresh mint leaves. The place did not promise a 5-star ambiance, but it definitely looked good enough, considering the situation I was in.

"Ek glass neembu paani dena, bandhu," I addressed people as bandhu when I was not sure about the salutation to use. I mean, when I was in Assam, dada was a universally accepted title; similarly, at most places, bhaiya would work. But in Mumbai, I was not sure whether it would be such a good idea to call someone bhaiya. So bandhu...

"Bada gilas ya chhota?"

"Bada de do." The headache was bada enough to order the 'bada gilas.' He fetched the water out of the pot using a wooden ladle, squeezed a lemon into the glass, sprinkled some mint leaves, and handed the glass.

I took a sip cautiously to avoid any surprises. I was surprised nonetheless but in a pleasant way. The liquid tasted wonderful. I popped in the Saridon and asked for a refill. Alcohol from last night had left me dehydrated; hence, some electrolytes in the form of lemon wouldn't have harmed. I took another glass and sat on the bench parked under the tree just besides the stall. The energy that was sapped by the incessant drinking last night was replenished to some extent. I was feeling much better now. Also, the Saridon had started working. The headache that was killing me 10 mins back was subsiding. I felt this was as good a time as any to enquire about the whereabouts of Nisha and Anjali.

"Hello Nisha, Ajit here..."

"Haa re bol... kaha hai?"

"Mai terminal ke bahar hu, tum kaha ho?"

"Pahuch rahe hai hum, Aisa kar Ajit tu gate ke paas rehna dhundne me aasani hogi, theek hai na, rakhti hu chal..."

"Ha theek hai, wahi rahunga... Bye."

I was glad that I had time despite the lemonade break. I walked up to the gate; they were not there yet, so I took my phone out to look at the pictures of Poorvi. There were memories associated with each of those pictures, memories that brought both a smile and a tear at the same time.

Watching her radiant face and the twinkling smile made my heart ache. I always knew the effect her voice had on me; whenever I was sad, her voice was enough to cheer me up. All my worries used to vanish in thin air when I saw her smile. I recalled how desperate I used to get just to see her once, just to listen to her voice, or for that matter, even to read her text. Anything even remotely associated with her brought a smile to my face.

Even after the final fallout between us, I was never actually able to give up on her; her place was still intact in my life. What made matters interesting was that this time around, she had gone the distance and openly expressed her feelings for me. I was surprised by her actions, to say the least, but at the same time, I was mighty pleased. It made me feel really special. Imagine when the person you've always loved comes forward and announces her feelings towards you; it is magical. Suddenly, I felt a strong urge to call her, to listen to her voice again.

I had my chance to talk to her just a little while back, but I blew it. I was dying to talk to her, but again, there was another conflicting thought that was holding me back. What would happen if I offer her my heart, and for some reason, things do not work out between us again? The only question was, was I ready to take the risk of undergoing the same pain that I underwent the last time we were together? Things had never been smooth and rosy between us ever, and there seemed to be a pattern in all the things that transpired. First, I do something stupid; she overreacts, promises never to talk again, then after some time, out of the blue, she calls and wants to get back together, and then the cycle repeats itself. My heart had been broken twice before. Was I capable of risking it the third time?

This was the biggest concern that was holding me back from plunging into the sea with her. I was busy weighing the pros and cons of calling her when I heard:

"Arre wo raha, waha dekh na... Ajeet." It was Anjali.

She was wearing a purple top with jeans. I must say this look really worked for her. I waved at her, acknowledging her hail, and walked towards their cab:

"Bahut wait karna pada kya, Ajeete?" Anjali asked.

"Nahi, 5 mins hua tha bas..." I said, walking up to their taxi to help them out with the luggage. After helping them load it on the trolley, I headed directly towards the counter to get our boarding passes. Except for a small delay waiting in the queue for security check, everything was smooth.

We boarded the plane, Nisha took the window seat, I took the aisle, while Anjali sat at the centre.

"Itna drink kyu karte ho tum?" Anjali said, fanning her nose with her hands. I must say her olfactory senses were incredible.

"Kaha? Mujhe to kuchh smell nahi aa rahi..." Anjali and Nisha were two different characters; Nisha had to be explained things, whereas Anjali was much more perceptive.

"College ka ek friend aa gaya tha usi ke saath..."

"Kitna piya? Bolna bolna, kaisa lagta hai?" I did not know Nisha was so curious. In office, she was the 'no-nonsense' person, and here she wanted me to fill in the details. I was a bit confused and also a little uncomfortable. Actually, I was never comfortable divulging the details of booze parties. But again, it was she who brought this topic up, so why should I feel uncomfortable about it?

"14 bottles tha... There were two of us, achchha tha, bahut maza aaya."

"Hatt, 14 bottles koi kaise pi sakta hai be... kuchh bhi," Nisha was finding it really tough to believe. I did not try to convince her by words; instead, I just smiled.

"Itna kyu piya... Khair it's your life," Anjali sounded concerned.

"Abe tu daaru pi sakta hai maine kabhi socha bhi nahi tha, mai to tujhe ek good boy samajhti thi," Nisha found it hard to believe that I could drink. I, however, thought that this reaction should have come initially when Anjali mentioned about me drinking for the first time, but again this was Nisha.

"Aapke sentence me do mistakes hai. First, maine daaru nahi pi beer pi and they are different. Second, drinking does not make anyone good or bad; it does not change your character," I was defending not just myself but all the other beer drinkers around the world.

"But still, it is bad for health na..." Nisha asked again.

"Aap google kar lijiye; you'll find the benefits of drinking beer. It's all out there," I retaliated.

"Arre chhodo bhi..." Anjali was annoyed by our discussion.

"Aee... chup reh tu," Nisha wanted to extract as much information on drinking as she could.

"14 bottle khatam karne me kitna time laga?" The interest that she was showing in my drinking was inexplicable. I decided to humor her.

"Soya nahi hu mai, abhi 2 hours pehle tak pi hi raha tha."

"Ha re college ki baatein karte karte time nikal gaya hoga," Anjali interrupted.

"Tujhe to interest nahi tha na..." Nisha said jokingly. They shared a great rapport and were always pulling each other's legs.

"Chup kar tu... Sahi bol rahi hu na mai Ajeete," Anjali wanted me to jump in.

While these two girls were trying to make the conversation interesting, I was still hung up on Poorvi. I glanced at Nisha and Anjali; it looked like these two girls could help me sort out my dilemma. I was in a place where some outside opinion would have helped a great deal.

"Ha, past recall kar raha tha. It kind of got nostalgic," I explained. I was looking for a situation where I could slip in the Poorvi topic without sounding weird.

"Kuchh hume bhi batao apne college life ke baare me," Anjali asked. This was the opportunity I was looking for. If I played my cards well for the next 5-7 mins, we could be talking about Poorvi by the end of it.

"College ke baare me kya batau... Just the way it is in all other engineering colleges, masti karna, class bunk maarna, aur ladkiyau ke kami pe aasu bahana..."

"Hahaha... Oye, teri girlfriend thi ya nahi?" Nisha interjected. It took less time than what I had expected.

"College me nahi thi..." I gave an open-ended answer, inviting another follow-up question.

"Matlab college ke bahar thi... Kaun thi, naam to bata," Nisha asked. Honestly, I had not expected this question from Nisha; I thought it would be Anjali. My opening was there nonetheless. I could now slide my little 'Poorvi situation' and have their opinion.

"Poorvi... Gangtok me we were neighbors," I pretended to be shy. I thought that this way, they'll take more interest in my love story, and it worked. Both Nisha and Anjali asked in unison:

"Abhi kya scene hai?" This was it; I could now pour in the details.

"Well... We were together for about 3 years then were separated for another 2 years, and as luck would have it, she called back again yesterday," I just filled in the points. I did not want them to know the details. After all, I was not saying this for their entertainment; I wanted an answer for my issue, and for that, those were the only things that they needed to know.

"Arre sahi hai Yaar... bahut saare sawaal puchhne hai tujhse, kaha se shuru karu, mai to kabhi soch hi nahi sakti thi ki teri bhi girlfriend hogi," Nisha's reaction was a bit over the top. Ideally, I should have been offended by her last comment, but knowing her, I knew that she did not mean it in a derogatory way.

"Matlab tu kya kehna chahti hai..." Anjali asked and then chuckled.

"Arre nahi re, matlab maine kabhi Ajit ko waise nahi dekha... Tu samajh raha hai na Ajit," Nisha added, defending herself.

"Koi baat nahi... I totally understand, shoot all your questions, I'm ready."

"Ye bata break up kyu hua?" Anjali asked.

"Bahut lambi kahani hai, thodi meri galti, thodi uski aur thodi halaat ki... Khair the important thing is that she called yesterday..." I said in such a way that made the reason for the break-up sound unimportant. I wanted them to focus more on the fact that she had called me.

"Sahi hai yaar... matlab wapas together?" Nisha asked.

"Nahi, it's not that straightforward... Thoda complicated hai. OK... now that we are on this topic I think I could use some advice," I said.

"Haan re, bol na..." "Haan, Ajeet, bol, kya problem hai?" Both Nisha and Anjali offered their help.

"Yesterday, Poorvi ka text aaya, and we started chatting."

"Haa, to problem kya hai?" Anjali asked.

"The problem is that today she said that she still loves me," I added. I knew they wouldn't be able to see the problem in this; I had said this just to get their reaction. It would have told me how interested they were in my story.

"Arre to isme problem kya hai?" Nisha wanted an explanation.

"Problem ye hai ki last 6 years me hum dono ka do baar break up ho chuka hai, and those breakups were brutal on me to say the least. Somehow, I managed to come out of the dumps, but I'm not sure if I can take the pain of another break up. However, it is not that I don't want to give it a try; I'm still hopelessly in love with her. Even when we were broken up, she was the only person I could think of. Please give your opinion on this, kya karu kya nahi karu soch hi nahi paa raha hu..." I explained my situation to them and asked for help.

"Dekh, Ajit, agar tujhe lagta hai ki tu usse abhi bhi pyaar karta hai to you should go for it. Chances of things working out are 50-50. Koi guarantee nahi hai ki this time things will work out for you two, but there is a chance that it may work out. See, the most important thing to do is to give yourself a chance to make things work. Agar try nahi karega to regret karta rahega, that too when the opportunity has presented itself before you. Agar ye opportunity nahi aaya hota to kuchh kehne ko nahi tha, things stood ended between you two but now chance hai tumhare paas... grab it," Nisha opined.

She did make a valid point; it was an opportunity that had presented itself, and I should not squander it. However, I needed a bit more convincing before I could commit myself. I looked towards Anjali, expecting her insight. I was kind of surprised that she had not jumped in in the first place itself.

"Dekh, Ajeet, eventually tujhe hi pata hoga what is best for you. It's you who suffered the agony of those breakups. You should consider one thing, though; if the risk pays off, just think what you will gain. The love of your life will be yours. Tumhe nahi lagta ki your love deserves another chance," she was right; the prize that was at stake was definitely tempting enough to put my heart on the line. I definitely would regret if I let this opportunity go by. In fact, I wanted to talk to her, I wanted to give it a chance, I wanted a life full of happiness with Poorvi.

"So, aap logau ka verdict hai ki I should accept her proposal," I asked.

"Arrc, Ajeet tu hi soch, kitne ladkau ke paas ye option aata hai... You are really lucky," Anjali made a valid point.

"Haa, Bandhu ye to hai... Infact I did feel special when I was proposed by someone whom I was in love with since eternity," I added.

"Haa re... It is special, ye important baat nahi hoti hai who is proposing, guy or girl. It becomes interesting when the person you love, comes forward and says those golden words. It is really really special," Nisha added in a dreamy voice, as if she was remembering someone.

"Nisha, kya baat hai... Bahut convincing sound kar rahe hai aap, kuchh personal kya?" I added cheekily, hoping to lighten her up.

"Chup kar re... Aisa kuchh nahi hai," Nisha replied, blushing.

"Bol na, Nisha... Ab tu aisa karegi? Bata na... Bata na..." Anjali started nagging her.

"Ajit jaisa long-term nahi hai, still..." Nisha caved in and started narrating her situation.

"Haa theek hai na... Bata na kaun tha?" Anjali asked.

"Mere engagement ke time, maine jab unko dekha tha." Nisha was blushing like hell... It was one of those Bollywood moments where the girl covers her face out of shyness... These are the moments that really describe a girl, and Anjali was there to pounce at her.

"UNKO?" waah waah... kaun hai wo... Naam to bata," Anjali asked tickling her. They were giggling.

"Sanjeev... my fiancé, actually I was floored when I saw him. Mai mann hi mann me pray kar rahi thi ki kaash ye rishte ke liye maan jaae," Nisha's face had become completely red, and she was smiling shyly.

"Oye hoye... Dekh kaise sharma rahi hai... Aisa lag raha hai ki Sanjeev babu yaha aa gaye ho.." Anjali was enjoying Nisha's situation, mocking her, making fun of her, tickling her. It did lighten things up.

"Aur jab unhaune rishta accept kiya to mai to pagal hi ho gayi... I mean aisa kitni baar hota hai, that too in arranged marriage. Baad me pata chala ki unke family totally agree nahi kar rahe the, Sanjeev ne khud insist kiya tab jaake rishta pakka hua..."

"Isiliye kehti hu Ajit, she has taken the first step this time, agar tum accept nahi karoge to believe me you'll regret it," Nisha added.

"Haa, Ajeete, aisa mauka nahi aata hai baar baar, ek baar chance le ke dekh, things will work out. Why are you just focusing on the negative side?" Anjali's comment kind of reinforced Nisha's point.

"With all due respect aap log ye bataiye ki why did it take 2 years to call back? What could be the reason? Achanak se pyaar jaag gaya?" I stated my concern.

Nisha and Anjali looked at each other with a small smile and then nodded their head ever so slightly as if they were saying 'typical guy.'

"Tu bataiyegi ya mai batau?" Anjali asked Nisha.

"Chal tu hi bata de." Nisha gave Anjali the go-ahead.

"What? Kya batana hai? Aisa kya hai jo ki itna obvious hai and I don't know." I asked.

"Hadd hai Ajeet, there is only one obvious answer to this, she was madly in love with you, something went horribly wrong between you two isiliye break up hua. She, however, was never able to forget you, she tried to suppress her feeling, she did it for the last 2 years, but with time the pain of losing you kept increasing, she called you when she wasn't able to take it any longer. Iska matlab ye hai ki she has completely moved past whatever it was that broke you two up. Ab wo tujhe kabhi khona nahi chahegi, from now on she will make the adjustments needed to make things work. These two years made her realize how much she loved you," Anjali's argument got me thinking.

"Are you sure... Nisha kya ye sach keh rahi hai?" I wanted to be sure.

"Haa re pagal, ladkiyau ki mentality tu nahi samajh sakta... Trust me Anjali is right, teri to lottery lag gayi hai," Nisha reaffirmed her statement.

"Thank you so much, both of you. Mai bahut confused tha, kya karu kya na karu... But thanks to you now I am decided." I was really thankful.

"Koi photo hai Poorvi ka, hum bhi dekhe usko jisne humare Ajeete ko pyaar karna sikha diya." Anjali started pulling my leg now. I had her picture on my phone, I showed it to both of them.

"Pagal hai kya tu?" Anjali punched me. "Ouch... Maine kya kiya?" I flinched.

"Dekh Nisha kitni sundar hai ye... Isse ye bhau kha raha tha," Anjali said, showing Poorvi's picture to Nisha.

"Arre re... sahi hai yaar... pagal hai kya tu. Land karte hi call karna tu isko... Iske liye agar tujhe Himalaya pe bhi chadna pade to chadh jaana re... Kitni sweet hai" Both Nisha and Anjali were impressed by Poorvi's beauty. Not their fault, she defined beauty.

"Point taken... First thing on landing I'll call her... I can't thank you two enough for dispersing whatever fragment of cloud there was in my mind."

"Maar khayega ab agar thank you bolega..." Nisha said jokingly.

I was glad I decided to take their opinion on this issue. Only a girl can understand the way another girl thinks. Now I wanted to talk to her as soon as possible, all the things that Anjali and Nisha said made me feel like a fool for having second thoughts regarding getting back with her. Over the next half an hour, we talked about how I met Poorvi, how Anjali ended up in the software industry. I learned that Nisha was a gold medalist in her college. Getting to know them made me realize how small and irrelevant I was; there are so many people in this world with such wonderful traits that you would like to stand up and salute them and their qualities. Finally, the plane descended and touched down at Bangalore airport.

"Ajit... call kar." We had not even alighted from the plane when Nisha demanded I call Poorvi. I had no reason to delay it. I took my phone out, searched for her number, and pressed the call button; my heart started racing. What would I say, how should I accept her proposal, what should be the tone, casual, excited, cool, aloof... I was working on all these questions when the IVRS at the other end took over, saying "All lines on this route are busy..." It was kind of an anticlimax for me. I tried again, still the same message; I kept trying for the next 5 minutes or so, with no luck. I was confused; generally, these days, network congestion is not seen in towns and cities, and yet I was not able to get through. Something did not feel right about this.

"Kya hua re? Phone laga?" Nisha asked.

"Nahi, network busy bata raha hai."

"Koi nahi, chal guest house se try karna."

"Hmmmm," I was starting to get a bit worried now. We headed towards the baggage reclaim area; I was still trying to get through the network but still there was no luck.

"Ajeete tension me kyu dikh raha hai. Guest house pahuch ke baat kar lena. Lagta hai bahut utavle ho rahe ho apne darling se baat karne ke liye," Anjali joked. I just smiled in response. We took our luggage, booked a cab, and headed towards our guest house. It took just a little under two hours for us to reach.

The long drive gave us enough time to know each other. Anjali was the one with all the jokes and leg-pulling, Nisha was more of an innocent type. I did not speak much; however, I was involved in their discussion and jokes. Most of those were directed towards me because of my silence. The long journey did not seem all that tiring because of all the merriment we were having in the cab. We finally reached the guest house, everything was in readiness. We were put up in adjoining flats. We went to our respective rooms to freshen up and rest.

"Shaam me chai saath peeyenge," Anjali said.

"Theek hai... Call kar dena please in case I doze off," I replied and shut the door behind me.

I switched on the television and started going through the channels, stopping at the first music channel, increasing the volume, and heading towards the shower. I had not slept for over 36 hours now, and the journey with hangover wasn't pleasant at all. My body was craving for some rest, but the journey from the airport till here had left me covered in dust from head to toe, so a quick shower was a priority. I took a nice long shower. I felt light, and all I needed now was a nice nap. I slid under the blanket and soon fell into a deep slumber. I was woken up by the ringing of the phone.

"Haaeeeellllllo," I said in a sleepy voice.

"Ajeete aaja chai peete hai..."

"Hmmmm kaunnnnn?" I was so deep in sleep that I was not aware of where I was.

"Anjali bol rahi hu... Uth jaa ab..." she replied.

"Theek hai..." I said, somehow I put down the receiver and went back to sleep. My sleep was interrupted, and I wasn't fully asleep, but at the same time, I was just a bit disoriented. I wasn't able to understand where I was. It was after some deliberation that I realized where I was; I slowly crawled out of bed, washed my eyes, and headed for the door. I was still very, very sleepy.

"Aao Ajeete, bahut soye..." Anjali remarked. I was too sleepy to reply; I just looked at her in affirmation.

"Call kiya?" Nisha asked.

I was so sleepy that I failed to understand what she meant, I asked in a confused tone:

"Kya? kisko?"

"Poorvi ko, aur kisko... Maar khayega agar bola ki nahi kiya hai," Nisha raised her voice.

"Arre ha re... Nahi kiya hai, just utha hu... Abhi karta hu." All my lethargy seemed to have evaporated just by Poorvi's mention. I took the cup and went to the balcony to call her.

"Yahi baat karna... Sharam aa rahi hai.... Ooohoooo," joked Anjali. I just smiled back at her and continued.

'All the lines in the route dialed by you are busy.' The annoying message kept on playing, I tried for another 10 minutes, still I was not able to reach her. I started to get a bit worried now; network congestion was a problem, but not getting through for so long was surely an issue as it doesn't happen always.

"Kya hua Ajit, pareshaan lag raha hai?" Nisha asked.

"Kuchh nahi... Bas phone nahi lag rahi hai." I tried to cover my anxiety but failed miserably.

"Kuchh nahi re... ho jaega. Kabhi kabhi network bahut kharab rehta hai." Nisha tried to console me, but I was too tensed to be pacified by her words. I sipped on the tea and switched on the television; I was browsing through the channels checking for some good-quality music. There was nothing interesting there. Nisha and Anjali were busy talking with each other. Suddenly a piece of news caught my attention:

Chapter 7

THE EARTHQUAKE

'High intensity earthquake shakes Sikkim, Sikkim Manipal Institute of Technology severely damaged.' was the newsfeed scrolling on the news channel. I couldn't believe my eyes; I went totally blank for almost a minute, just staring at the TV screen.

"Ajeet... Ajeeettt..." Anjali was shaking me, trying to bring me back.

"Haa... ha... kuchh na... mai theek theek..." I wasn't able to speak; I was literally lost for words, and nothing I said made any sense.

"Ajeet shanti se baith tu abhi... kuchh nahi hua hai," both Nisha and Anjali were fanning me, but I would not stop perspiring; it seemed as if someone had spilled a mug of water on my head.

"Yaar mujhe usse baat karni hai... baat karni hai yaar... There are a lot of things that I need to ask, bahut kuchh kehna hai mere ko usse Anjali... Yaar ye kaise ho sakta hai... Will I get a chance to talk to her again, baat kar paunga kya mai usse kabi Nisha, bol na... please..."? I was completely hysterical.

"Arre tu ghabra mat, drink some water," Nisha handed me a glass of water.

My hands were shaking; I was not able to hold the glass properly. Anjali helped me with the water. A few minutes and a couple of glasses of water later, I finally settled down. I tried her number again, but with no luck; every time it was the same annoying voice at the other end.

"Suggest something, kya karu mai abhi?" I asked this of both of them.

"Abhi kya kar sakta hai tu Ajit, dekhna usko kuchh nahi hua hoga, she would be fine." Anjali tried to console me, but deep down, I'm sure even she feared that the worst might have happened.

"I hope that everything is fine, but is there any guarantee about it? What if I never get to see her again, Anjali? Usne mujhse aaj subah hi kuchh bataya tha, and I did not acknowledge that. Yaar, how will I be able to live with this thorn in my chest, ek baar baat karne ka mauka mil jaae bas, just once, Anjali... I want to talk to her just once." I was just desperate, and in this desperation, I was just blabbering, almost turning a deaf ear to any kind of logic.

"Magar kar hi kya sakta hai tu, we can just pray during this moment of crisis," Nisha said. I stayed quiet for a while, analyzing the viable options that I had, then suddenly I thought out aloud:

"Yes... Mai jaa raha hu, mai jaunga Gangtok jaunga."

"Kya bol raha hai, pagal ho gaya hai kya? Abhi sab public waha se bahar nikal rahe hai, aur tu waha jaane ki baat kar raha hai. Thoda logically soch," Nisha sounded her disapproval.

"Ha Ajeete, Nisha sahi keh rahi hai, thoda sensibly soch," Anjali supported Nisha.

"Nahi, agar mai abhi nahi gaya to mai kabhi chain se nahi reh paunga. Mujhe usse milna hi hai." I was not able to give any reasonable argument, but again doesn't love defy logic...

"Waha jaake tu karega kya?" Nisha asked.

"Aur office me kya bolega? Hume special assignment de ke bheja gaya hai. Career bigad sakta hai tera if you take this step," Anjali tried to scare me.

"Agar Poorvi hi nahi rahegi to mai career ka kya karunga. Anjali, please understand one thing, she is my life; uske bina mera career kisi kaam ka nahi hai. I am going ahead with this." I was sure about this; there was nothing that could scare me now, I had made up my mind. My argument had an impact on both Anjali and Nisha, I thought.

"Tere emotions ka mai respect karti hu, but I feel that you should give it a second thought. Jo hona tha wo ho hi chuka hai; do you think you would be of any help there?" Nisha was still skeptical about my going.

"I may not be able to help, but I think my presence will be a big boost for her. Ek hypothetical situation de raha hu, god forbid but say if somehow you break your leg, the damage that was supposed to happen has happened, it can't be reversed right? But how would you feel if you see Sanjeev by your bedside in the hospital, can you describe the ecstasy that you'll feel then? Won't you appreciate that gesture forever?" Both Anjali and Nisha were quiet; I thought they would support me now.

"I understand your concern and I am really moved by it, but this is the moment where I should be with her. I should be able to help her, comfort her, and make her feel protected in whatever way I can." The point of me being there at her time of distress overpowered any other argument that would have stopped me from going. "Kya bolti hai Nisha? Should I go?" I asked again.

"Haa re ja... magar khayal rakhna abhi waha bahut problem hoga." Nisha was finally on board.

"Thanks."

"Maar khayega agar thanks bola to," Nisha said, I could sense her voice choking.

I was occupied by just one thought, Poorvi and her well-being. I was filled with regret because of the fact that I had failed to reciprocate the feeling which she had expressed towards me. I came back to my room and latched the door; I did not want to be disturbed and switched on the TV. I wanted to gather as much information as I could about the quake, and what I saw was really depressing. It measured 6.8 on the Richter scale; it was intense enough to cause a lot of destruction. Plus, the fact that this had hit the hills made it worse. If initial reports were to be believed, the casualty would be in hundreds. North Sikkim was worst hit; I was a bit relieved as SMIT was in South Sikkim. This relief was as short-lived as possible because almost immediately they started broadcasting the images from SMIT, and the pictures looked bad. The damage was extensive; actually, the quake had triggered a rockslide, and it had literally crushed the beautiful college. It had been 3 hours after the quake, and the media was bringing in live pictures from the scene.

The rescue operation was severely hampered because of the constant aftershocks, and the army had not managed to cut through the debris. It was after some 20 minutes or so that the first footage of the affected area was broadcast.

It showed a couple of army men bringing a body out. It was drenched in blood; the face was so battered that it would have been impossible to recognize it. The fact that these images were shown on national TV was a bit strange, but it gave me an idea how bad this quake was. I remembered I had the number to Poorvi's shop; I tried to call there but again the same annoying voice at the other end greeted me; it seemed impossible to get through the network. I had many school friends there; I was in touch with a couple of them, so I tried calling them but again no luck. I was trying to keep all the negative thoughts at bay and focus on the trip that I was planning. Nisha and Anjali were right when they said that things were going to be tough. Considering what I was up against, I had to plan my actions immaculately, but I was not in a position to think clearly, so I decided to bring in my friends from PZ in the loop. I was sure they would have something helpful. I took my phone out and typed the message:

'Guys, reached Bglr... One prob though. Kal maine Poorvi ke baare me bataya tha, she is in Skm, waha earthquake aaya hai and her coll is badly hit. I am going to visit her. Any inputs?'

'Pagal hai kya saale, waha abhi mat jaa bahut ganda situation hai waha pe,' replied Suman. I wasn't expecting this from Suman; he was someone who was a perfect embodiment of sacrifice for love.

'Gadha hai saale tu, ladki ke liye waha jaega saale, pata hai kitna dangerous hai? Chup chaap kaam kar apna,' came Mishra's reply. Well, I had expected this from him.

'Senapati go ahead, make things right this time; you should go there at least as a human being if not as a lover. Sab theek hoga,' Shantanu replied.

Nobody except Shantanu advised me to go to Gangtok. Everyone who replied was genuinely concerned for my well-being, but I was expecting something positive, something that would push me further. I knew the main reason for their skepticism was the fact that they were not aware of the backstory between me and Poorvi. Had they been aware, they might have been more supportive.

'Ha be Shantanu, thanks...' I was about to hit the send button when I got a call from GKD.

"Ha bhai bol," I tried to mask my anxiety.

"Sun... Tera msg padha, kya hua, tu sach me jaa raha hai?" GKD wanted to know for sure whether I was serious about going to Gangtok.

"Ha yaar... I have to go, I have to be by her side."

"Pakka soch liya hai? Matlab waha bahut problem face karna pad sakta hai." GKD stated the obvious. The way he said it sounded as if he was building ground for something else, something serious.

"Ha yaar soch liya hai... There is no turning back now," I reaffirmed my desire to go.

"Chal theek hai, agar soch hi liya hai to I am with you."

"Thanks be..." This was the first set of positive words I had received without having to explain myself; this strengthened my resolve, I was more determined now.

"Sun... tu kaise plan kar raha hai jaane ka? Matlab Kolkata hoke hi jaega na?" GKD asked. I was not sure why he was asking me this. What I knew for sure was that he wouldn't have asked me this if there wasn't something important or relevant that he had to offer.

"Ha, but if I can get the direct flight to Bagdogra I'll go there directly," I answered; Bagdogra was the nearest airport from Gangtok; however, the frequency of the flights was low, so I might have to break the journey at Kolkata.

"Chal theek hai, jo bhi karta hai mujhe bata dena. Please late mat karna, jaise hi flight book karega mujhe bol dena," GKD made this strange request; it sounded unlike him. There was something he had planned that he was not revealing. I, however, did not think much about it.

"Chal theek hai, bata dunga," I replied.

"Pakka... Immediately." His inexplicable interest in my plans was baffling, but there were other things that had occupied my mind and needed prior attention.

"Ha bhai, ekdum immediately," I said, totally unaware of his plans. I disconnected the call, sent the message that I had typed for Shantanu, and sat down at my computer to book the tickets. As I had expected, there were no direct flights to Bagdogra. This meant I had to break my journey at Kolkata. I did not have any other option, so I went ahead and booked the tickets. Upon receiving the booking confirmation, I called GKD.

"Oye GKD... ticket kar liya hai, Bangalore to Bagdogra via Kolkata." I was still unaware of why he was so interested in my flight.

"Achchha... kaunsa flight hai? Timing?" GKD wanted me to fill him in with the details.

"Spicejet-SG528 Bangalore to Kolkata, 9:55 in the morning, waha se connecting flight hai Spicejet-SG323 Kolkata to Bagdogra 13:55." I was still trying to figure out why he wanted the exact details about the timings.

"Theek hai, sahi hai... Aur bata." He sounded weird; it seemed he was busy doing something else, and the 'Aur bata' was an attempt to stall me.

"Theek hu... kuchh khaas nahi... tu kya kar raha hai." I asked in a circumspect tone.

"Ho gaya... mera bhi ticket book ho gaya." GKD exclaimed.

"Kya? kaunsa ticket." I was confused; what was he saying?

"Abe tu kuchh bhi bol magar mai apne liye kisi aur problem me nahi daal sakta."

"Abhi bol diya to bol diya, magar aagey se kabhi ye mat bolna. Saale 4 saal hum saath rahe hai. Does that mean nothing, tu mere jagah pe rehta to kya karta. Tickets book kar liya hai maine, there is no looking back from here. Chal saath chalte hai aur bhabhi ko dhund ke laate hai," GKD ended the sentence with a cliché.

"Theek hai re bhai... Thanks bolne ka mann ho raha hai be, but at the same time gaali bhi dene ka mann ho raha hai. Tu bahut emotionally react kar raha hai. Khair agar tune decide kar hi liya hai to phir kya bol sakta hu, milte hai kal." I knew GKD from college; if he was anything, he was stubborn. He would not commit himself to something, but once committed, there was no 'looking back.' Probably it explained why he used 'no looking back' so often.

"Chal bye... Milte hai kal. Tu zyada tension mat lena. I have a gut feeling things would be ok." GKD tried to console me.

"Chal bye... Thanks yaar." I thanked him.

After disconnecting the call, I sat on the bed trying to come up with a strategy for the journey. The toughest thing that I would have had to face was that I would be entering an area that has been hit by an earthquake. Apart from the 'natural' obstacles/difficulties, there would be another problem: the rescue team would not let me in. However, I thought to tackle this issue as and when it came. First, I had to plan for the journey. I knew the terrain would be hostile, and I should make sure that I carried minimum luggage. Keeping this in mind, I started packing, only the 'essential' stuff. I was packing when I heard the doorbell ring. I opened the door, and Anjali was standing on the other side. I was surprised to see her. We had already discussed whatever had to be discussed, so was she here to try and talk me out of going to Gangtok? If she was here for that, I wouldn't take it anymore. I was prepared to give her a piece of my mind if she said anything against me going to Gangtok.

"Hi Ajit, kuchh baat karni hai... Andar aa sakti hu?" She asked for my permission in a low but serious tone.

"Ha, please come in."

"Dekh Ajit, regarding the discussion we had at tea..." This tripped me off, it left me fuming. Why in the world was she so concerned about me? I was aware of all the consequences, yet I wanted to go, so why was she so bothered? In a fit of rage, I interrupted her and in a very decisive tone said:

"Dekh Anjali... Let me save you some time here. If you've come to tell that I should not go, well... I'm going, and nothing, absolutely nothing is going to change that."

"Nahi Ajit... Mai tujhe rokne nahi aayi hu. Infact, I want to apologize about my behavior back there. I back your decision, and regarding the office, tension mat le. We'll manage something, even if it means working extra hours, we will do it. Tu bas bina tension ke jaa, but ek baat ka khayaal rakhna, things are not going to be easy out there. Apni safety kabhi compromise mat karna." Anjali said. I felt bad for being rude to her. I had reacted a bit too soon. She meant well, and I was glad she supported my decision to go and was also grateful that she offered to cover for me in the office.

"Thanks, Anjali. You can't understand how big a relief this is for me. Thanks again."

"Koi nahi Ajeete, packing kar liya, aur kaise jaa rahe ho?" She inquired.

"Wahi kar raha tha. I'll be taking only the essentials; more luggage will only slow me down. Flight book kar liya hai, yaha se Kolkata jaunga, waha ek aur friend join karega, then from there Bagdogra. Waha se struggle shuru."

"Who? I mean who will join you?" she asked.

"Gautam Kumar Das, he was my hostel mate. I tried to convince him not to go, but he wouldn't cave. He tricked me into giving him my flight details, and then he too booked the tickets." I answered.

"Sahi banda hai yaar, jo tumhare liye itna bada risk le raha hai."

"Haa, pagal hai gadha..." I added with a smile.

Only I knew how much his gesture meant to me.

"Ok, you finish your packing... let's meet at dinner," Anjali said before leaving. I packed all the necessary items in a small backpack. It was done in a jiffy; there wasn't much to take anyway.

After I was done packing, I switched on the television. I wanted to gather as much information as I could. All the news channels were showing the catastrophe that had hit Sikkim. It had been just three hours, and aftershocks were being felt. Images of panic-stricken people were being broadcast at regular intervals. The extent of damage could not be estimated as yet. However, based on early estimates, the casualties could be in hundreds. North Sikkim was hit the worst of all the places. Poorvi's college, Sikkim Manipal Institute of Technology, was in South Sikkim. It was quite far from the epicenter, but the quake had triggered a rockslide, which had damaged the college the most. Listening to the news feed, I realized how difficult it was going to be to enter the affected area. We won't just have to fight nature, but also have to overcome the resistance put forward by the rescue team. There was no way they would just let us in. It would be only logical on their part. I mean, during times of disaster, people are not expected to enter the affected areas. Those guys were there to evacuate as many people as they could to safety. I had to get into that restricted zone somehow. I was trying to find a way that would facilitate our entry when I heard a knock on the door. I checked my watch; it was well past 9.

I had completely lost track of time. I walked gingerly towards the door and opened it.

"Sir khana laga diya hai," it was the caretaker of the guest house.

"Theek hai, aa raha hu," I replied. I was so engrossed in my thoughts that I had completely forgotten that it was time for dinner already. I took a quick shower and headed for the dining area. Nisha and Anjali were already there, probably waiting for me to start.

"Kaha tha... Phone dekh," Nisha said in a complaining tone. I took my phone out; there were a couple of missed calls from her.

"Sorry, I must have missed it while I was in the shower," I explained.

"Chal chhod khana khaate hai, bahut bhook lag rahi hai," Anjali seemed to be in some sort of hurry.

I sat down quietly next to Nisha at the dining table; the food was good, but my appetite wasn't all that great. There was a deathly silence at the table. I was too preoccupied to talk, Anjali probably felt offended by my cold attitude towards her, and Nisha might still have been dwelling on the fact that I had not received her call. Whatever the reason, there was silence; the only sound was that of food being chewed. After a while, the silence turned into awkwardness. I was trying to find a topic that would ease the tension, but the more I thought, the more difficult it became to start a conversation.

Finally, Nisha broke the silence and asked: "To Ajit jaa raha hai tu..." It was more of a statement than a question.

"Ha... Subah nikal raha hu," I replied.

"Tujhe pata hai Nisha, iske ek friend bhi jaa raha hai iske saath..." Anjali said.

"Kya baat kar rahi hai, sach me kya?" Nisha asked, turning towards me.

"Ha... maine bahut mana kiya magar wo maan hi nahi raha hai. Pehle usne mera travel details maanga, then mere flight me hi ticket book kar liya usne," I explained.

"Sahi hai na Nisha, aise friends hai... Tu bahut lucky hai Ajeete," Anjali reminded me how lucky I was to have friends like the ones I had.

"To kya plan hai, kaise jaega?" Nisha asked; this time she sounded serious.

"Flight hai yaha...."

"Arre flight details nahi chahiye, ye bata Gangtok enter kaise karega?" Nisha interrupted before I could finish my sentence.

"Well... Abhi kuchh decide nahi kiya hai, but we'll figure out," I answered.

"Abe tujhe pata hai kitna tough hoga... Aise situation me tu kaise ghus paega, military won't allow you to go." It wasn't something I didn't know already, but again the fact that she was trying to discuss the problem was worth appreciating.

"Ha, problem to hoga, but Gautam and I will figure something out." I didn't have any great plans as of now but was confident that when the time comes, I would have something concrete. I, however, had thought of a backup final resort.

"Kuchh to soch ke rakha hoga," Nisha was persistent.

"Ha, soch ke rakha hai, but you know nothing concrete yet... kuchh keh nahi sakta." I had a little plan in place but had to pull a few strings to put the plan into action.

"Chal theek hai, I hope tera plan kaam kar jaae. But make sure you have something concrete planned before you leave." Nisha cautioned.

"Ya..." I added with a smile. Another ten minutes and some chit-chats later, we finished our dinner.

"Koi chai piyega?" Anjali asked.

"Pagal hai kya? Tea at this time?" Nisha questioned.

"Mai to hamesha dinner ke baad peeti hu, tujhe peena hai to bol," Anjali said.

"Order kardo... I'll join you." I had already packed my backpack; the night was still young, and there was nothing much to do. Also, all this while I had been thinking about Poorvi and the earthquake. I had to think about ways to enter Gangtok, something I could not do with my mind preoccupied with these thoughts. I needed a clear mind to think effectively. I thought spending some time with these girls, sipping tea, and chatting might help me.

I asked the caretaker to get us two cups of tea.

"Mere liye ek coffee." Both me and Anjali turned towards Nisha sporting a wry smile on our faces.

"Aur nahi to kya mai khali baith ke kya karungi," Nisha filled us in with a smile.

We spent another couple of hours chatting. I had agreed to have tea at this time just for one reason, and that was to clear my mind of all the negativities. After a while, the conversation lost its energy, the words were marred by frequent yawns, out-of-context laughters, and misplaced words. All of us were tired, but no one was willing to concede that sleep was catching up. We were desperately trying to stay awake, picking on small fragments of conversation.

Finally, Anjali's words bailed us out of our agony: "Chal yaar, sote hai ab... Tu bhi aaram kar Ajit."

"Haa re chal... bahut late ho gaya, tu kitne baje niklega kal?" Nisha asked.

"9:55 pe flight hai, 8 baje ke aas paas niklunga," I replied.

"Theek hai yaar, ek baar mil ke jaana."

"Haa yaar, mil ke jaana... Ab chalo, bahut neend aa rahi hai, good night," Anjali said, showing unprecedented haste.

"Good night," I said and headed towards my room.

I was drained of all energy; I felt so weak that I didn't even bother to take off my slippers. I just jumped into bed face first on the pillow.

I was tired, no doubt, but I couldn't sleep. There was so much going on that it was impossible for me to get any sleep. I lay there for a few minutes without moving, without thinking. There was nothing that could hold my thought; one moment I was thinking about the earthquake, the next moment about Poorvi, and the one after that about the beautiful moments I had spent with her—the breakups, the patch-ups, the events that transpired last night, the morning messages. I could barely hold on to any thought for more than a minute. All these thoughts made it all the more difficult for me to sleep. Unable to sleep, I sat up on the bed, trying to figure out ways to enter the estranged region. I tried my best to find ways that could lead me there.

Obviously, there was one problem in planning: I was nowhere near the actual site. I was not aware of the possible problems that I may have to encounter there. All I could do was speculate from here. Still, I thought good speculation was better than sitting idle and going there just to get surprised. After brainstorming for a while, I remembered that one of my school seniors was working with a leading news channel. I had even forgotten his name; I was not able to concentrate properly. Many things were going on in my mind, and it probably was not ready to start another thread of processing. However, I did not give up; I tried my best to concentrate. I had strained nearly all the cells in my brain. As it always happens, just as I was about to give up, I remembered his name, 'Karma'—one of the most common names in Gangtok, and I could not remember it. I sprang up in anticipation; he definitely could pull some strings and get me inside Gangtok. Now all I had to do was get in touch with him. This was not as straightforward as it sounded. I had never had any contact with this guy. Still, I knew him; I had heard about his achievements. It was simple, as people who did not know him personally were still aware of his achievements. It was a big deal not just for Gangtok and its people but for the whole of Sikkim. There were not many people from Gangtok or, for that matter, from Sikkim itself who could say that they have had the opportunity to be on television. Of the many things that I regretted today, I had to add one more thing to it—I had lost contact with all my school friends.

To say that I had lost contact would be sugar-coating; I had never bothered to stay in touch with them. They, on their part, had tried to continue the association and take it as far as they could. I, on the other hand, never acknowledged their efforts; instead, I deliberately avoided them. If that was not all, I stopped taking their calls and never returned their messages. Eventually, their persistence wore off, and they too stopped trying. If only I could go back in time and undo my mistakes, things could have been easier for me now. I had lost an arrow from my quiver; however, all was not lost; there still was one option left—I could ask my uncle to try and get in touch with their family. I remember him mentioning the 'Kalzang' family more than once; in fact, he was invited to Karma's marriage. He could definitely help me get in touch with him. There was one problem, though: how would I talk my uncle into giving me Karma's number? As far as I know, he was aware that I had never had any business with Karma or, for that matter, the Kalzangs. I was so excited about him that I had overlooked the most important fact—my uncle was just one of the links between me and Karma; he was not directly linked to him. In fact, I doubt if he would recall Karma by his name; to him, he always was 'Mr. Kalzang's son.' I looked at my wristwatch; it was past midnight. This brought a two-fold problem with itself. First, my uncle would be fast asleep, so my story had to be effective enough to justify my calling him at this hour of the night. Second, he would have to call up their parents or some other acquaintance to get the number. Again, he would have to explain to them the hurry and why it could not wait till morning.

Both these issues could, however, be tackled if I came up with a strong story justifying my call. This solution I felt, in itself, was a problem for me. I mean, cooking a story credible enough for both my uncle and his contact to buy was not a small task, considering the state of mind I was in. However, I had to cool myself down and get to work; time was of the essence, and that was one thing I did not have. I was feeling suffocated in the room; there was too much going on in my head, and the closed space did not provide enough oxygen to think clearly.

It's not that I did not have any ideas coming through; they were coming but were not good enough considering the situation I was in. I toiled for an hour or so, but nothing good came up. There was no story that could endure the brunt of one simple straight question: 'But why do you need Karma Kalzang's number specifically?' The ideas that I had so far were of the order of inquiries at best, like "My boss's relative/friend was in Gangtok, on hearing the news of the earthquake he is really worried, so he wanted to inquire about him." There was no way this story could fetch me Karma's number. There was nothing strong that I was able to come up with, so I was left with no option but to fall back on the classic, tried and tested style of lying. The golden rule is that keep the things as original as possible with just a subtle change. I could tell him my exact situation just replacing myself with my boss and Poorvi with his relative. This was an option; this could work for my uncle. But again there was a problem; if he did not have Karma's number, he would have to call Mr. Kalzang, and I am not sure about the impact my story would have on him. There was no point throwing this story; in all probability, it stood to get shot down by Mr. Kalzang if not by my uncle.

I was lost for ideas; there was nothing I could think. All the ideas seemed to start from me calling Uncle and ended by those getting shredded by either Uncle or Mr. Kalzang. Seeing no other option, I decided to do what I did best—act at the moment. There had been many instances where I found myself in some sort of tricky situation where any amount of planning did not help. I always confronted those situations head-on, right on the face, and more often than not, I was triumphant. So be it, this was one such situation; I had to summon the courage and the attitude of past Ajit. There was no point sitting and thinking about ways to fool Uncle and

Mr. Kalzang into giving Karma's number. I should go there and face the situation.

I had used up all my energy, still nothing good came out of it. I was still at the same point where I started. I decided that I should try to get some rest; sleep had eluded me all this while. Still, I wanted to lie down, and if I got lucky, sleep would also come. I glanced at my watch; it was already past midnight.

Things were gloomy, but again I could not afford to go down the same road again. I knew nothing good could ever come up from that. But one crazy thing about the human mind is that the more you try to avoid something, the more it catches on to you. There is practically no avoiding it. I tried to think about things that were not related to her, things that would not remind me of her or of the tragedy that she finds herself in. But somehow, I ended up mapping her to everything I thought. I started off by thinking about college life and all the frolics I had there, but in the end, after a minute or so, I ended up thinking about the days I spent with her, the nights I spent on the rooftops talking to her, how I braved the cold during those winter nights, how those laughters were enough to shake off the effect of cold, how we spent the weekend together in Kolkata, how we had broken off, how she had called me yesterday, how she expressed her love for me, and how I blew her off.

The moment this thought entered my mind, I became restless. I started cursing myself for my stupidity; I should not have left her hanging. After all, I was as much in love with her as she was with me, if not more. Again, I sat up, and I knew whatever I did, I wouldn't be able to sleep. I knew there was nothing that would help me get her thought out of my mind. There is something called the guilty conscience, and probably I was suffering from one of those nerve-wracking situations.

Whatever I tried to think, I ended up with the same old thought, how I had shut her down when she came up to me with her heart on a platter. The thought that there was a possibility that I might not get to meet her ever again was all the more troublesome. I always knew that this was a possibility, but I never let my mind wander in that direction. But again, how long could I have left my mind oblivious to this fact? I knew I was past the ignoring phase; I had to face the reality and consider all the possibilities. Till now I never allowed my mind to tell me that Poorvi might not have survived, but now that I was open to this idea, my resolve to get there only got stronger. I could not wait to face whatever came in my way; I was not going to flinch; I was going to make it, no matter what. Suddenly, there was an unexplainable rush of energy. I couldn't wait to start the journey; suddenly, all the negativity seemed to have evaporated away.

Sleep was miles away from the lid of my eyes; however, the lethargy that had crept inside me was long gone. I was feeling an unprecedented energy, and it was impossible to sleep when blood in that volume is rushing through your body at speed. I was no longer low on energy, and I had had enough fresh air, so there was no reason for me to stay out. Plus, the weather was getting a bit chilly. I decided the best thing to do right now was to get in bed and try to stabilize myself; after all, there was a big and arduous journey ahead of me. Uptil now, my only focus was on going to Gangtok and finding out about Poorvi's well-being, but now that the entire event had sunk in me, I was able to think more clearly and take different aspects into consideration.

One thing that I had not considered, or rather, one thing that I had ignored till now, was that it was a dangerous expedition to undertake—dangerous as in 'fatal'. There was a chance I might get engulfed in the wreckage and be another count in the casualty list. No doubt it was not a war, but still, the danger was there. It wasn't that I was getting scared or anything; in fact, my resolve wasn't shakable; I stood firm on my decision. Actually, what this thought did was it gave me an insight into life. I wanted to soak in as much of Bangalore as I could before I left. I looked around to see the beauty of nature. All these things were there all the while; I had just not stopped to appreciate them. I was too consumed. But now suddenly everything seemed beautiful—the moonlight casting its milky spell on the trees and the open surroundings, the silence of the night all felt different now. I was busy thinking about the beauty of nature; this had a really calming influence on me; the rate at which my heart was beating slowed down; my worries seemed to have subsided. I thought I might go and get some rest; dawn wasn't a long time away, but still, I went in to bunk inside the warm blanket. I was now able to see things much more clearly; I realized how clouded my thoughts were back then and how it hampered my decision-making. The reason for the hazy thoughts was that I wasn't able to take into consideration all the aspects, all the possibilities, and all the outcomes. Now that I was considering all the possible things, I was much more matured in my actions. I lay there going through these things in my mind, and with those thoughts doing rounds in my head, I don't remember when I fell asleep.

One of the most annoying sounds in the world woke me up—the sound of my alarm clock. I checked the time; it was seven, and I was supposed to leave by eight. Luckily, I had my default alarm set at seven. I was in such a deep slumber that in all probability, I would have overslept and missed the flight. I got up, rubbing my sleep-filled eyes, and headed towards the bathroom. After I had cleaned up, I took my backpack that was packed from last night and headed towards the girls' room to bid them a final goodbye.

On reaching the door, I rang the bell; it was 7:45 in the morning. I was sure that these girls would still be sleeping. So there was no reason for me to expect an instant answer; I waited another couple of minutes before hitting the bell again.

"Abhi nahi bhaiya, baad me aana," one of the girls shouted from inside; I wasn't sure which one. They probably mistook me for the caretaker. I thought of shouting back, but again, it would've disturbed other residents, and also, I wasn't very comfortable shouting, so I typed a text instead: 'It's me Ajit... Leaving for Gangtok, just wanted to say bye' and sent it to both Nisha and Anjali as I did not know who it was who had shouted back.

I glanced at my watch; it was 10 mins to eight; the cab driver was already waiting for me, and it didn't seem logical to wait there, so I started walking away. Right then, I heard the door knob click and open. I turned back to see who it was; it was Nisha, she was a complete mess, drunk with sleep, she could hardly keep her eyes open. She had opened the door with her right hand, and with the left palm, she was rubbing her eye as if trying to rub off sleep from her eye.

"jaa raha hai..." her voice was so deep, soaked in sleep, that I kind of felt bad waking her up.

"Ha... bas nikal raha hu... Socha mil ke jaata hu," I replied.

"Ruk mai Anjali ko bulati hu," she said and walked back into the room before I could say anything. After a couple of minutes, Anjali came to the door.

"Baahar kya kar raha hai? Andar aaja," her face looked even more 'sleepy,' those eyes of hers were swollen, not 'cry' swollen, but just been woken up from sleep swollen.

"Ab andar aa bhi jaa," Nisha said. I was already getting late, and she was telling me to come in. Come in for what?

"Ha... arre nikal raha hu, bye bolna tha. Actually, I'm already running behind schedule," I replied. I was really getting late.

"Chal yaar... All the best, aur kya bolu. Bas tu yaha ke tension se free rehna. Hum sambhal lenge," Anjali said.

"Haa re... Tu bas apna khayal rakhna aur call karna," Nisha also added. They looked genuinely concerned.

"Achchha... koi help chahiye hoga to call kar dena, don't hesitate... Apne taraf se jo bhi ho sakta hai hum karenge." Anjali was trying to provide me a cushion, and yes, it felt good knowing that someone had offered help in case I needed it.

"Thanks Anjali... Mazak nahi kar raha hu, but this is very comforting... Thanks," I said. After Anjali was done, I looked towards Nisha, I was expecting that she'll have something useful to say.

"Yaar bas apna khayal rakhna aur jald se jald kaam khatam karke waapas aa jaana," she said. Her concern for me was not completely expressed by her tone. I knew she meant well, but the sleepiness in her voice kind of eclipsed her concern.

"Theek hai bandhu... Chalo nikalta hu, Dua me yaad rakhna," I said these final words before leaving.

"Chal bye..." both said together.

I turned and walked away without looking back. This was a symbolic gesture because I had made a resolution that starting now there will be no looking back.

I knew what I was walking into; I was going to a place where difficulties stood there with extended arms, and I had to somehow avoid running into them. However, all those difficulties that were in store seemed to be minuscule considering that I was going to meet Poorvi; running into an earthquake-hit area for this seemed a petite thing. I could have jumped into a volcano to rescue her if such a time came. People use the phrase 'Love Of Life,' but she wasn't that for me; she was just 'Life' for me, and anything that I would do to save her would, in fact, be a step towards saving myself. I was being overtly selfish here; I loved my life, and there was no way that I would let it go without putting up a fight. I was also determined to succeed no matter what; now, either I go there, or I get nowhere.

These thoughts worked me up really good; I was beaming with confidence even though I did not have any plan, any backup, any story that would help me get inside the affected area. In spite of all these loopholes, I still was confident because I had a friend with me, a friend who was selfless enough to come along. With him around, I was confident that things would be good.

I walked down to the parking area where the cab was parked. Looking at the cab, I couldn't help but remember the cab ride I had yesterday.

Things had changed so much in the last 24 hours. Yesterday, the only problem I had was figuring out what to do with Poorvi's proposal. In fact, it wasn't so much a problem as it was a reaction out of my displeasure towards her forfeiting the relationship 2 years back. But today, things had changed in the worst possible way. Today, I have accepted her love for me, but a larger and much more dreadful picture loomed large ahead of me, and it was her safety, and that was the only thing that mattered today. The driver came out of the cab and opened the back door for me. I tossed in the bag and hopped inside. Thinking about Poorvi and her texts yesterday pulled me down a bit, but again, this wasn't the time where I could let negativity set in.

Chapter 8

THE FLIGHT

I was busy contemplating the situation at hand when my phone rang.

“Ha bol bhai,” I answered the call.

“Yaar tu nikal gaya na?” GKD asked.

“Ha yaar, cab me hu... May be another half an hour and I’ll be at the airport,” I answered.

“Abe daru piya hai kya? Angrezi me bol raha hai,” GKD joked.

Any humor, good or bad, was like gold for me. I knew one thing about myself: if my mind was thinking clearly, I’d be shooting for gold. So I decided to humor him.

“Ghanta daaru, raat bhar excitement me so nahi paaya...” I added with a laugh.

“Chal theek hai phir tera time kharaab nahi karunga, so jaa cab me,” GKD said, I wasn’t sure whether or not he was serious.

I reached the airport barely on time, and I had to make a dash towards the terminal to get my boarding pass. After the security check, I relaxed a bit and went inside the lobby to wait for the boarding announcement. There was some time to kill, so I took my phone out and started reading some old messages. Soon I realized it was a bad idea, a very bad idea; it brought back memories, memories which reminded me of Poorvi and the present situation. So I started browsing through the stalls, and after a couple of overpriced sandwiches and a bottle of coke, the announcement was made. I walked towards the said gate number and moved with the queue to enter the plane. I was allocated the middle seat, it was a two-hour flight, and I had to find ways to keep myself occupied.

I didn't have a good sleep last night, so I thought the best way to kill time would be to catch a nap. The flight took off on schedule, and I had already made myself comfortable on the seat. Honestly speaking, I did not care who sat besides me, so I didn't even throw a glance to find out who they were. I closed my eyes and started counting my breaths. I had heard people say that this induces sleep, and frankly speaking, I saw their logic. What else would you expect when you are actually counting the number of times that you've breathed?

I was busy counting when suddenly I saw an army officer, tall, broad-shouldered, mustached, and rugged. I couldn't understand his business here; what the hell was he doing in the plane, all dressed up in full uniform?

His personality was such that once you saw him, you just couldn't unsee him. He sat in an upright position; his posture suggested that he was a ranking officer, the look on his face showed that he had something important on his mind, and he looked dedicated to the task at hand. I was awed by the man's personality and was practically staring at him. Suddenly, he turned and caught my eyes; this was kind of embarrassing, so I turned away. After a while, I turned to check if he was still looking at me. Well, he was, and not just that, now his face was twitching with anger. I thought I was in some real danger; however, I didn't know why he was so angry at me. I was just looking at him; I wasn't sure why this bothered him so much. This man was so big that he could have killed me with his bare hands, and to top it all, I had nowhere to run. I was stuck in a closed capsule, left at the mercy of this scary guy.

I started sweating, thinking about the trouble that I was in. Why did I have to look at him in the first place? Now I had pissed him off. I looked at him from the corner of my eye; I think he saw me again. He stood up and started walking towards me. There was no running away from this situation now, so I stood up to face him. This might not have been the brightest thing that I could've done, but there was no other option. There was no way that I could've avoided this monster who was prowling towards me.

With every step that he took towards me, I prayed that somehow he realized that an armyman was supposed to save and protect the welfare of common men and not hurt them. But that didn't happen; instead, he came and stood close to me and with a stern, authoritative voice he asked:

"Kya dekh raha tha?"

"Kyu nahi dekh sakta kya?" If my constant staring wasn't enough, I was sure this would've ticked him off.

My words made him so angry that his face turned red, nostrils started flaring, eyes widened, and the veins on his forehead started popping. It looked as if he had reached his breaking point. And then, in a fit of anger, he held me by my collar and said:

"Chal pahucha deta hu tujhe jaha jaana hai tere ko."

He dragged me by my collar along the aisle and headed towards the door. I was trying to shout, but for some reason, I just couldn't speak. It seemed as if I had turned mute. The fact that nobody was protesting this atrocity made me think whether I had even turned invisible.

I didn't know what to do; the collar of my shirt had made a solid grip around my neck, and he was dragging me with it, choking me. Everything around seemed so different. Was my staring at him such a bad thing that I was being treated this way and that nobody was protesting?

Meanwhile, the savage there wasn't willing to let go. He seemed hell-bent on proving his words right:

"Chal pahucha deta hu tujhe jaha jaana hai tere ko." But again, how the hell would he know where I was going? Just then, I realized where I was going and why I was on this plane. This didn't help the mysterious situation that I found myself in; instead, it presented before me a whole new plethora of unsolved, unexplained situations.

While I was flummoxed at the bizarre developments, the angry armyman was dragging me over the floor of the aisle towards the door of the plane.

On reaching the door, he said:

"Chal yaar, thoda masti karte hai."

My mind was going berserk; this was the first time that he had said something in a relaxed voice. What did he mean by 'Thoda masti karte hai?' He, or rather I should say we, reached the door of the plane, and there he stopped. I looked up at him in complete disbelief. I just couldn't understand what he was up to. That bloody bastard was just smiling away, and quite inexplicably, I could sense a childish innocence in that smile. Was I crazy? How could I see the innocent side of someone who had held me by my collar and was dragging me towards the door of the plane?

I looked at him and then at the door. What was he going to do? Was he going to throw me off? Was he crazy enough to even try to do this? He reached for the handle on the door. The smile was still intact, and with the same innocence, he said:

"Ajit chal yaar, milte hai Poorvi se."

I was terrified. How did he know either me or Poorvi, and how did he come to know that I was going to meet her?

Everything around me was a big mystery that was deepening every minute. Just then, he broke the door open and pushed me out. I was floating. I wasn't scared; I just felt as if I was swimming in the air. Mid-air, I saw a hand held out towards me. I reached out for it, but it disappeared, only to reappear again as a face—the face of Poorvi.

Seeing her, I welled up. I couldn't explain her presence there, but I was overwhelmed seeing her.

"Poorvi..." I said.

"Pakad lena... Please... Der mat karna," said Poorvi. Her face transformed back into a hand, and I reached out to hold it, but it disappeared. Seeing this, I started crying out loud.

"Sir... What's the matter? What is it, sir?" A lady was speaking out to me, and the person sitting next to me was shaking me.

"Kya hua... Are you OK?" The person beside me was asking. I did not know what was happening there; I was lost.

"Poorvi was there... The door..." I was feeling disoriented and was trying to get the people's attention towards the door by gesturing towards it.

"Sir... It's ok, nobody's there. Probably you've had a nightmare or something of that sort," the lady said.

It was only after a couple of minutes that I understood where I was and what exactly had happened. I was in a plane and had dozed off; there was no armyman, no Poorvi, and well... I was safe.

"I'm sorry. The last couple of days have been really rough on me; I must have had a bad dream... Sorry," I apologized to the air hostess and the person sitting next to me. Everyone went back to minding their own business, and I was left to think about the dream I just had. Did it mean something?

I started putting the pieces together; there were two phrases that had stayed back with me: "Chal pahucha deta hu tujhe jaha jaana hai tere ko" and "Pakad lena... Please... Der mat karna." I was sure it meant something, but I wasn't able to get to it. Was my seeing an armyman some kind of an indication or something? Based on the first impression, I thought that the armyman was GKD. The way he kept saying, 'Tujhe waha pahuchaunga jaha tu jaana chahta hai' reminded me of how he had offered to help me in my endeavor. Actually, it was immaterial who or what the armyman symbolized. What was really significant was the part where I saw Poorvi and when she said: 'Pakad lena... Please... Der mat karna.' Did God, in his infinite wisdom, want to send me some signal regarding Poorvi's well-being?

I wasn't the type of person who believed in dreams and then acted in response to that, but the stakes were too high to ignore anything. In fact, I was in a position where anything concerning Poorvi became a matter of utmost priority to me. I knew it was just a dream, but somehow those words that she said kept echoing in my mind. What did those words mean? My worst fear that I kept from surfacing was standing and staring at my face with its fangs hooded at me. After the dream, I started aching, and the ache was for Poorvi. The memory that I had about her was quite old; it had been two years since we broke up, and since then, we had never run into each other. Now when I saw her like this (even though it was just a dream), it made me feel as if she was physically present alongside me. My heart started racing, and I was feeling as restless as I ever was.

Amidst all this restlessness, I was trying to infer the meaning of her words when an announcement was made, saying that the plane would be landing at Howrah terminal in around 20 minutes. I was glad, and glad for two reasons:

1) I was getting closer to my destination.

2) I'll have a companion for the rest of my journey. I reclined back in my seat and tried to relax while I waited for GKD.

After around half an hour, I saw a tall guy with a small black backpack enter the plane. It had been 2 years since I had last seen him.

He had changed a lot in this period. The last I saw him, he was this skinny guy who looked almost like a cloth hanger. His tall stature made him look even thinner, but I guess time had done its trick. He had now put on some weight; he kind of looked hefty. One thing that had not changed though was his specs. He was still holding on to that round golden frame, which kind of added at least a couple of years to his age.

"Abe yaar sahi hai be Ooozeeet," he said in his trademark style. So there was one more thing that had not changed, the way he called me Ooozeeet.

"Abe kelaa GKD... Mota ho gaya be," I couldn't help saying it.

It was one of those moments when you forget everything that has been bothering you. Right now, all I could think of was how in the past 2 years we never met. I'm not particularly proud of this, but the agony and despair that had enveloped me just a while back was gone, or at least it had taken a back seat and it wasn't bothering me right now; for some strange reason, I was feeling light.

"Abe hum dono ka seat bahut dur dur hai..." He looked at his boarding pass and said.

"Rook baat karta hu..." I said, standing up.

"Abe tu baith, mai baat karke aata hu." It was typical GKD; he rarely let someone else do things for him.

He went towards the attendant and probably started presenting his case. After a while, he started talking to someone else, a fellow passenger. Maybe he was looking for a mutual settlement. I was hoping that we'd sit together for the rest of the journey. This way, we would have the opportunity to chalk out a plan. I knew we were not on a jolly ride, and the only thing that could've guaranteed our success was our preparedness.

GKD returned after some 5 minutes and said, "Ye seat waala maan gaya peeche jaane ke liye."

"Sahi hai be..."

"Aur bata kya chal raha hai? Feeling any better?" GKD asked.

"Yaar bahut zyada feel good to nahi ho raha hai, but I'll bounce back..." I replied with a smile.

"Oye... Shantanu kaisa hai? He has completely gone off our radar." GKD asked about Shantanu.

"Sahi hai yaar wo, kaam me thoda busy rehta hai. Parsau raat bhar piya hum dono ne, maza aa gaya kasam se. Baal bahut dinon se college waalon ke saath baitha nahi tha. Maaka... aisa lag raha tha jaise wapas college pahuch gaya," I couldn't help but smile as I replied, probably because it reminded me of the good time I had with a friend after such a long time.

"Sahi be, college ke bhi kya din the... Koi tension nahi, koi problem nahi. Infact waha pe biggest problem hota tha lunch ke baad class karna, proxy me pakda jaana, attendance manage karwana. Iske alawa problems kya tha be? Aur ab dekh har roz targets meet karna, apne ideas ko kaise project kare so that it is appreciated and at the same time, it remains 'my' idea. Maaki aankh, yaha to ab har dusre din mere efforts ka credit koi aur le jaata hai. Saala kabhi-kabhi sochta hu kya isi kiye padhai kiya tha."

Gautam Kumar Das, this name meant something back in college; he was one of those guys who was rarely ruffled come whatever may. This monologue that he just gave was the last thing I would have expected to hear from him. But again, time does change you in unspeakable ways.

"Haa re...Time makes us dance to its tune. Ab maine ye kabhi nahi socha tha ki kisi din mai office me bina bataye, bina family ko inform kiye kisi ladki ko dhundne nikal jaunga, and the biggest issue of all is that I am not sure if..."

I couldn't complete the sentence. It wasn't that this thought had never come into my head; it was just that whenever it came, I pushed it down. I had never talked about it before with anyone else. Probably this was the reason why my eyes went all misty when I actually said this.

"Abe tension mat le... Sab theek hi hoga." I just nodded. I knew he was trying to console me; he, however, knew this well enough that I was in a place where these words of consolation were of no use to me. At the same time, I knew he was just being courteous. I had known him long enough to understand that he was perceptive enough to gauge the situation, and those words were nothing but an effort to try to calm me down.

What followed was a small session of awkward silence. I was still thinking about Poorvi, and GKD was probably trying to come up with something appropriate to talk about. The silence was broken by the announcement made by the captain of the plane; he wanted us to fasten our seat belts. After the announcement, it was silent again. After a little while, when GKD could no longer take the awkwardness, he spoke:

"Yaar sun, we can avoid talking about it, but that wouldn't be the correct approach. We have to come up with a plan so that we can get inside the affected area. There would be a lot of obstacles there, and not just natural obstacles. We'll be stopped by the rescue workers. At every step, our presence there will be questioned, and there is no way that we can go the distance without something concrete planned."

He had a point. I should have had something concrete planned out, but I did not have time at hand. Also, my thinking ability was crippled by my emotional outbursts.

"Haa be... Kuchh to plan karna padega. I wasn't in a frame of mind wherein I could've come up with something that would've been helpful. Hamesha sirf ek hi baat sar me ghoom raha tha, how I blew her away when she had opened her heart to me." I accepted my mistake, and recalling it made me weak again. These frequent breakdowns were doing me no good. Right now, I was losing it at the drop of a hat, and there was nothing that I could have done to help myself.

Amidst all this, there was one consolation for me; I was not alone. I had someone who was there to help me in case I broke down again. Also, the mettle to come up with something interesting wasn't on my shoulders alone. There was someone who could share this load with me, and I trusted him more than I trusted myself. I was sure he would come up with something intelligent, something that would get me to meet my love.

"Abe sahi hai yaar... Now you have one more reason to give in your best to reach there, and whatever may come, there should be nothing that should shake your confidence. Baal, jaenge aur usko dhund ke laenge. Chahe jo ho jaae, tu bas ghabrana mat." It was obvious that GKD was trying to boost me. I also realized that he did not know why I was so desperate to go to meet Poorvi; he was completely unaware of the situation, which made his gesture all the more commendable.

"Haa be, akela rehta to shayad thoda darr jaata magar ab nahi..." His presence meant a lot to me; a long journey without someone alongside you can be really demanding, and I was more than happy that this issue was taken care of.

"Khair chhod. Bata kaise jaenge... I think we should start planning," GKD got down to business.

"Ok... Abhi we'll land in Bagdogra, waha se nikal ke Siliguri jaenge..." I mumbled; actually, I didn't have anything else worked out till now.

"Matlab we don't have a plan at hand, koi baat nahi abhi sochte hai," GKD said.

"Abe sorry yaar... Mai kuchh soch nahi paa raha hu... right now I was in a place where my mental faculties had kind of given up on me."

"Chal theek hai, I can understand your frame of mind; I know it's difficult for you to concentrate right now with all the things going on." GKD patted me on my back, almost consoling me, and then he continued:

"We should start by taking into account the possible difficulties and the obvious roadblocks ahead. Ek ek karke problems identify karte hai phir uske baad unke solutions nikalenge." He said and went for his backpack and pulled out a black hardcover diary; it was the same iconic diary that he carried with him while we were in college. As the training and placement member, he used to keep a list of all the companies that he had contacted, their response, and the date he last talked to them, and also what was the last response. Now, with that diary in place, I was sure about one thing: things were going to be methodical from this point on. He took a pen out and started scribbling with it on the diary. "First of all, we need to arrange a vehicle; it is obvious that there won't be any public transport available that'll take us to the affected area. Koi gaadi to chalne se rahi. That was the first entry in the roadblock section. Achchha ye bol Ajit, koi hai Siliguri me jo ki tera help kar sake." I started thinking; the first name that sprang to mind was "Bikash." We were classmates, but then this was a long time back. I wasn't in touch with him, I guess for the last eight years now.

True, at one point in time in school, we were inseparable, but now I wasn't even sure where he lived or what he did. Even with all these uncertainties, he was my best bet, as there was no one whom I knew in Siliguri who would actually even consider helping me.

"Haa yaar, ek banda hai... I think wo help bhi karega. We were in school together, but there is one problem though: after school, we've kind of lost touch. Still, I think he's our best bet, and maybe our only bet." I knew if I met him, he'd definitely help me in every possible capacity.

"Chal theek hai... We'll call this plan A, but we need another one in case this doesn't work out." He was in his elements; I knew whenever he starts using phrases like Plan A and Plan B, he means business. I was confident that with his planning and my steely resolve, we would make it through. I just sat idle, waiting for him to suggest a "plan B," and there it was:

"Siliguri me kuchh hire kar sakte hai? I think kar sakte hai... Yesss... chal ab to vehicle ka tension khatam, ye idea thoda costly hoga, but it's a sure-shot option, no doubt." This was typical GDK; he would come up with some idea, assess its credibility, and then applaud his effort.

However, I was glad he was there because he brought with him a method that promised one thing, if not anything else, and it was that by the end of the journey, we would have taken into account nearly all the possible problems that could've sprung up. I knew him well enough to know that he wasn't done by any stretch of imagination; if anything, he was just getting started.

He continued:

"Ab hume at least ek vehicle mil gaya hai. Now let's focus on the next problem. Arranging a vehicle is not a solution to anything unless we figure out how we should enter the region... Koi raasta hai?" GKD asked me; I thought GKD was doing one of those bits where he used to ask a question and then answer it himself.

"Abe kuchh to bol, kaise jaenge?" GKD asked again after I did not reply.

"Abe ruk, soch raha hu," I replied.

I thought for a while and then remembered that there was one way that might be unguarded:

"Yaar ek raasta hai; I happen to know one route. It is relatively longer, and people do not prefer that for commutation. I think that area will be less dotted with security personnel and rescue workers." I suggested. However, there was an inherent problem in this plan; I assumed GKD would get it, hence I did not read it out to him. This was my journey, no doubt, but GKD was the most important component and the only companion, and I wanted him to feel useful all the time.

"Abe wo to theek hai, magar ye bata wo raasta kitna damage hoga? Because let's face it, we don't want to tread a path where there won't be anyone to help us in case we land ourselves in trouble. One thing's for sure, there's going to be many such instances." Like I had guessed, GKD got a hold of the situation.

"Haa be, this is a problem, but then I guess we'll have to take the risk. All those routes that will have any sort of population will attract the rescue workers, and that is one thing I think we should avoid. It will be really hard to explain to them why we want to get there." I tried to defend my proposal.

A frown grew on GKD's face, and after a couple of minutes of silence, he said:

"Ek baat bata mujhe, Ajit, why are we trying to avoid the rescue workers?"

"Because they won't let us in." I replied in a single sentence.

"Tu clearly nahi soch raha hai, even if we avoid the rescue team here and enter the borders of Sikkim, what will that accomplish?" he asked.

I was confused at the beginning, but after thinking for a moment, I realized why he had asked this.

"Haa be, I had not considered this angle," I replied.

"Abe what angle, I can't just assume that we are on the same page. If you've got the angle, spell it out. Ajit, I want answers right now, not just replies." GKD was in his element; the way he got all worked up at this slight slip-up of mine reinforced my belief that he was there with me and willing to help me with all his strengths.

"Sorry, I understand that you are concerned over the fact that even if we enter Gangtok, we'll have to eventually face the people we were trying to avoid all this while. We'll have to enter the college, and there will be no shortcuts or secret routes that'll help us get in there. I also understand that it'll be much more heartbreaking if they won't allow us or for that matter evacuate us after reaching there, so I think we should find an alternative or at least discuss the option of bringing the rescue workers into the loop early." I gave a detailed description of what I understood and how we should proceed forward from hereon.

"Abe senti kha gaya kya? Tu to jaanta hai ki jab mai planning karta hu to aisa ho jaata hu. Sorry yaar agar tujhe bura laga." GKD thought that I was hurt, and this reply was motivated by that emotion.

"Abe nahi re... I understand that whatever you are doing, you're keeping my best interest in mind." I explained I was not upset or angry; instead, I was obliged.

"Chal agar tu theek hai, to planning resume karte hai," he said.

"Haa yaar please..." I agreed.

"Dekh, let's discuss the options at hand:

We go by your plan, take the deserted route, reach the place, and then tackle the hindrance that shows up there. This idea is not all bad; it has one positive point. Agar hum college ke paas pahuch jaenge to convince karna easy hoga. The rescue team ka ek hi concern hota hai, to stop people from getting into danger. Now if we reach that place, then they may allow us to go and find Poorvi." GKD now seemed to have an inclination towards my plan.

However, there was one problem or a situation or, to say, a fact that seemed to have been overlooked. Our entire plan was leading us to Poorvi's college; it seemed that we were going to either accept or reject our plans based on its feasibility of taking us there. I do not know what made us think or, to say, conclude that Poorvi would be trapped in the debris of her college; she might very well be at her home.

"Abe GKD, ek baat sun, I think there is a big flaw in the way we are approaching this entire situation," I wanted to attract GKD's attention to this point.

"Bol kaise?" GKD was busy analyzing the plans that we were discussing earlier; he probably thought that I couldn't have anything constructive to add here.

"Why are we focusing all our energy on how to reach Poorvi's college, matlab aisa bhi to ho sakta hai ki she is with her family. I mean we'll be visiting the affected place after over 24 hours at least. Tujhe lagta hai ki Poorvi waha hogi." I explained.

He immediately looked up from his diary on which he was busy scribbling words. There was a look on his face that clearly said how surprised he was. He didn't say a word, just nodded in agreement. Seeing that he was still trying to soak in the feasibility of the point I had put forward to him.

"Arre haa re... This is a valid point, baal pehle kyu nahi socha humne. Abe yaar, we've missed valuable time raking our brains over something that was not going to yield any results or at least positive results." GKD looked clearly upset for overlooking this point.

"Yaar koi nahi... Let's not lose ourselves. If we plan keeping in mind that we have to reach Gangtok and visit her house, things will be easier." I did not want to lose GKD at this juncture. No doubt he was a calm fellow, but he became very fussy when his plans seemed to be flawed because he overlooked some scenario. I needed his calm demeanor to guide me.

"Haa chal theek hai, koi baat nahi. The first step of this plan will remain intact irrespective of where we want to go. Now that we have to reach Gangtok, I think we should take the route that you had mentioned earlier. Now we do not have the problem of running into the rescue workers, kyuki the residential area ko fully evacuate nahi karenge. College me to pakka kisi bahar waale ko ghusne nahi dete," GKD said; he was back to his normal analyzing self.

"Haa yaar, but before we decide on the plan, we should discuss all the possible pitfalls that we expect to encounter." I didn't want to jump to conclusions before having analyzed all the possibilities.

"Chal theek hai, tu kaun se 'pitfalls' dekh raha hai," GKD replied. He did not sound all that pleased, plus the way he used air quotes for "pitfalls" highlighted that he was not totally comfortable right now. He was probably dwelling on the fact that he had overlooked an important factor. I was a bit offended by those air quotes, but I did not want to upset him further. So, ignoring the comment seemed to be the best and most intelligent thing to do at that time.

"See, taking any route is not a problem for me. I also understand that this route would increase our chances of reaching Gangtok, however..."

"What 'however'?" GKD interrupted before I could complete the sentence.

"However, the path will be risky. The very fact that this path wasn't often used even in its heyday is a thing that draws my attention. The terrain must be difficult, and also, do you think that this earthquake would have spared that route? What if we get ourselves into trouble there? There would be no one to help us out. Leave that; there would be no one to even hear our pleas in case we cry out for help." I made my point.

"Matlab tu darr raha hai... Sahi chutiya hai tu, agar darna hi tha, to yaha tak aaya hi kyu?"

I don't know why, but GKD was acting really weird. I was offended by the way he kept snubbing me.

"Abe nahi re... Mai darr nahi raha sasuri, aisa kuchh nahi hai jo mujhe dara sake. Maa kasam, tujhe lag raha hai ki mai apna well-being Poorvi se pehle rakhunga. Maa kasam, sasuri, mai tere liye soch raha hu, behenchod, mai tujhe apne liye to problem me nahi daal sakta na." I was really upset because he thought I was afraid.

"Abe nahi re... Mere liye tu tension mat le. Saale, mai tere saath aata hi nahi agar mujhe peeche hatna hota. Tu jitna daredevil hai, mai bhi utna hi hu. Ab risks ko account me lete hai, magar we should not drop any plan just because it's too risky. Ek baar jo maine commitment kar di, phir to mai apni bhi nahi sunta." GKD joked; it was his genuine attempt to lighten things up.

"Chal theek hai... But as usual, we should have a plan B." I added; having a plan B for everything was the way GKD worked.

"Haa... Plan B to rakhna padega hume, but I don't have much idea regarding the terrains and the hostilities associated with those places." GKD was finally thinking right.

"Haa, theek hai, I understand why I should take this responsibility, but I do not see any options we have for our plan B. According to me, there is just one thing we can do in case we decide not to implement plan A. We'll have to use our 'people skills' to get inside the borders. If that works out, there could be nothing better. We'll have the help and support of the people who know what they are doing, and our entry will become so much easier." I was emphasizing the positives of plan B. I was hoping somehow we could find a way that would make the execution of plan B easier.

"Ajit, mujhe aisa kyu lag raha hai ki tu plan B ko plan A banana chahta hai?" GKD asked point-blank.

"Dekh bhai, I am not trying to force anything; I'm just saying that we'll strike gold if somehow we manage to convince someone there to help us." I replied.

"I take your point, but tu khud bata what is the possibility that we can have them help us."

"Yes, I understand the odds are low, but do you think that you should abort a plan because the odds are stacked against us? Mai kya keh raha hu, let's start with this plan first because then we'll have the second plan to fall back on. However, if we start by taking the deserted route, we won't have anywhere to fall back to in case something goes wrong there." I explained why I was avoiding taking the deserted path.

"Chal theek hai... It seems you've thought this through; iske against mai kuchh nahi bol pa raha hu. Aisa nahi hai ki mai tere points ko kaatna chahta hu. I just want to analyze every aspect before committing to anything."

"Abe tu bhi saale... I know whatever you do, you'll be doing it keeping my best interest in mind." I was never bothered by the constant cross-examination that GKD was doing. I knew very well that his intentions were good.

"Abe ye bata kisko target karna chahiye?" GKD asked after thinking for a while. Before I could answer, the pilot made an announcement saying that we'll be landing at the 'Bagdogra Airport' in about 15 mins.

"Abe tera karma bhoomi aa raha hai," GKD added with a laugh. I replied with a smile. This was really a 'karma bhoomi' for me. But as the minutes passed, my anxiety started growing. It was because there were still a lot of loose ends that needed to be tied before we could commence on the trip and expect it to be successful. The trickiest thing was that we were running against time.

"Abe kya hua, tere smile me tension ka subtitle dikh raha hai?" GKD sensed my anxiety.

"Nahi re... Tension nahi hai, magar hum Bagdogra pahuch gaye hai, aur abhi bhi bahut saare questions hai jiska koi answer nahi hai." I explained the reason for my anxiety.

"Hieght case patti hai tu, saale negative side kyu dekh raha hai, ye soch humne kitna progress kiya hai." He tried to console me.

"Chal theek hai, magar nikalne se pehle apna plan of action jot down kar lete hai, kya bolta hai?" I suggested.

"Theek hai, likh... First hume Bikash ke paas jaana chahiye. I think we should bring him in the loop; he'll definitely have something to help us. Second, on the way, we'll have to find who can help us to enter the place. Third, we'll have to come up with a story potent enough so that they would fall for it and agree to help us." I dictated.

"Theek hai, likh... So, tujhe bikash ka address pata hai na?" GKD asked.

"Haa... Yaad to hai, but it's been over eight years, memory thoda hazy hai, but I think it's not completely gone."

"Koi baat nahi, ye ek chance lena padega. Agar kismat saath diya to mil jaega wo. Else tu hi soch, what are the chances that he'll be at home?" GKD said.

The way he put those words made my heart sink. I was really banking on Bikash and was hoping to find him. The odds of finding him were already low, and now after GKD's explanation, it seemed even more difficult.

"Oye gadha... Kya aadmi hai be tu, kuchh bhi baat hota hai tu saale muh latka ke baith jaata hai. Ye kya baat hui?"

"Abe nahi re... Bas thoda soch raha hu."

"Ghanta soch raha hai... Saale sochna hai to ye soch, jab humne ye journey start kiya tha to kya us waqt Bikash picture me tha? Ab agar wo milta hai to bonus, aur agar nahi milta to kya, we'll think that he was never in the picture." GKD did make sense. Why brood over the loss of something that was never with you in the first place?

"Chal theek hai, ek baar jaake check kar lenge. Mila to sahi hai, else we have alternatives." I replied.

"Chal landing bhi ho gaya. Shanti se nikalte hai, auto karte hai aur dekhte hai kismat apne saath kis hadd tak hai." GKD said. We alighted the plane, and the air hostess smiled at me at the gate and said 'take care, sir.' I knew it was because of the antics earlier.

We did not have any luggage with us; all that we had were our backpacks, hence there was no waiting at the baggage claim area. We deboarded the plane and walked out through the exit. I headed towards the pre-paid taxi counter.

"Abe kaha jaa raha hai?" GKD asked.

"Cab book karne," I replied.

"Cab kyu? Teri girlfriend hai kya yaha pe?" His choice of words surprised me; he was fully aware of the situation I was in and yet he chose those words.

"Abe sorry yaar... Dhyaan nahi diya," GKD realized his mistake.

"Arre koi baat nahi, chalta hai. But cab book karu?" I asked. I did not know why he did not want me to book a cab.

"Sun yaar, pehle hi bahut kharcha ho gaya hai tera, and this is not the end. Aur bhi bahut hoga, so I think you should be judicious in the way you spend," GKD explained. He was right; I should not be looking for luxuries right now. There was a bed of thorns awaiting me, and here I was looking for a comfortable, luxurious ride.

"Haa yaar, sahi bol raha hai. Let's go outside; I think we can hire a tuk-tuk there." I suggested.

"Koi city bus nahi chalta hai kya?" GKD asked.

"Shayad chalta hai, but the problem is that I am not sure whether I'll be able to recognize the stop. The bus driver's coordination can be difficult, so I think we should go for a tuk-tuk. Plus, it is not very expensive either." I clarified. So we decided to take a 'tuk-tuk'. The decision was made so both of us headed towards the exit. I took my phone out and switched it on. I decided to call up Anjali and Nisha to update them about my situation here.

"Hi, Anjali... Ajit here."

"Ha, yaar bol... Pahuch gaya? Dost mila? Koi problem to nahi hai?" She had a lot of questions, and she did not hold back shooting them at me.

"Anjali cool... Theek hu mai, abhi airport se nikla, GKD bhi mil gaya hai. How is everything there?" I asked.

"It's all good here; koi tension nahi hai. You take care of yourself," Anjali replied.

"Chal theek hai phir... Thanks again, gappu... Rakhta hu, will keep you posted." I said and hung up.

Chapter 9

FINDING BIKASH

"Dada, pradhan nagar jaabo?" I asked in Bangla; this way, the auto driver wouldn't come to know that we were not from here.

"Hae... Kintu pradhan nagare koithai?" The driver asked where in Pradhan Nagar.

This was an awkward moment. I wasn't a confident Bengali speaker. So I started framing some sentences in my mind and checked if they were appropriate. I was thinking of some sentence and then scrapping it all over again; this took a lot of time without me realizing it. Eventually, the driver lost his patience and started yelling:

"Tara tari bolo kothai jaaba? Jadi tumi bolte paro na, aama ke chhari diyo." Speak quickly, where do you want to go, or just leave me.

"Dara. Ae ki chitkaar, ha... Aami bolchhi to." I told him to stop his yelling. This time I did not have to think of the correct words to use; it happened spontaneously, and luckily all the words that I used were authentic Bengali words.

"Sevok road theke petrol pump aasse to... Oi theke ek ta road bazaar bhitore jaachhe, oi roadet jaaete lagbo," I replied.

"Hae... aami bucchhi... chalo," the cab driver got an idea where I wanted to go.

"Koi taka?" I asked for the fare.

"Pochis taka manush," 25 per person. I did not know what the correct fare was. What I knew was that it rarely happens that you are told the correct fare by the cabbie.

"Na na... Pochis taka nai, kuri taka manush dibo." I offered him 20 rupees per person.

GKD gave me a stern look. I knew I was bad at bargaining and I must have made another bargaining blunder.

"Pain...talish taka diye diyo, chalo." The driver relaxed his offer to 45 rupees.

"Na na, kuri taka manush chhara ek taka beshi debo na." I told him that I was not willing to pay him a penny more than 20 per person.

"Basho..." The driver signaled to sit.

"Hieght case hai yaar, tujhe bargaining karna nahi aata hai." GKD said, and the driver looked at us from the rearview mirror.

"Abe chhod... Let's hope wo mil jaae hume." I replied.

"Achchha, ab we should resume our plan." GKD told, pulling out the diary from his backpack.

"So, this is what we had decided to discuss on our way to Bikash: Zero down on the person who could help us get inside Gangtok, come up with a story that's convincing enough for that person to allow us and even help us in getting there." He read out the contents from the diary that he had written on the plane.

I had a doubt in my mind but was too scared to bring that up. Why should we wreck our brains coming up with a story? We had a story with us, or should I say a fact with us. Why couldn't we say that we are going to check the well-being of my girlfriend? However, I also knew that I was not in a place where I could think clearly and rationally about this entire episode, so I decided to go by GKD's judgment.

"Kisi media waale ko pakad sakte hai," I suggested.

"Army waale ko kyu nahi?" GKD countered. I knew this counter was in good spirit. He was not the type of person who would start an argument just for the sake of it.

"Because when an army personnel takes up any job, the first thing that they do is shut down their emotions. They never let emotion influence their decision. It would be next to impossible to try and soften them." I explained why I had suggested we go with the media.

"Tera explanation to sahi hai, but I think even media personnel won't have full authority there. As far as I know, even they have to produce a pass or something in order to get entry." GKD pointed out the flaw that was there in my plan.

"Ok, on one hand we have people with authority but we don't have a good story, and on the other, we have a good enough story but no authority." I summed it up for him.

"Haa, what do you think will be easier, coming up with a story that will convince the army men or entering the region relying on someone with limited authority?" GKD asked for my view.

It was a difficult choice, and there was nothing certain with either option. What I really thought was that we stood to lose whether we opted to go with the media or with the army. There was no way we could enter the place, I thought.

"Abe ab aise put kar raha hai to lagta hai ki army hi option hai." I surrendered.

"Arre mai dishearten karne ke liye nahi bol raha tha. Tu jaanta hai, before reaching any conclusion, I thoroughly analyze all the possibilities. Aisa bhi ho sakta hai ki koi media waala humara help kar de. I'm not saying these things to derail you from your path." It wasn't that I had ever doubted his methods.

"Oye patti insaan... Tujhe lagta hai ki I resent your arguments? Sasuri, I know whatever you're doing you're keeping my welfare in mind." I wanted him to realize that I was the last person who would doubt his intentions.

"Ok, then it's good. But we still have that problem looming large over us. What do you say?" GKD wanted me to take a stand or at least give a logical opinion.

"That problem is still there, and there seems to be no escaping it. But again, kuchh to nikalna hi padega. Baal abhi kucchh soch nahi paa raha hu." I expressed my inability to come up with something useful.

"Chal koi nahi, mai kuchh sochta hu." GKD said that he would take over. This was a big relief for me.

"Dada, Sevok road aaslo, gali bhitore jaite lagbo?" The driver said that we've reached Sevok road and whether he should take the 'gali.'

"Hae... Bhitore chalo." I told him to take us inside.

"Yahi kahi iska ghar tha... Zyada dur nahi. I remember because we used to play for hours together at this field." I said, pointing towards an open space. Earlier, this used to be a playing area, but now that 'field' was filled with garbage and broken asbestos pieces.

"Oye... Yahi utar jaate hai, auto me baithe baithe we could miss his home. What do you say?" GKD proposed that we deboard the 'tuk-tuk' and walk our way towards Bikash's home.

"Ha, this sounds good. Zyada dur nahi hai, some 400-500 meters, I guess." I supported.

"Dada ruko... Humko yahi chhod do." I asked the driver to stop, deliberately in Hindi, handed him the money, and started walking.

I had never thought that after all these years this place would get me nostalgic. True, I did have a lot of memories associated with this place, but all that was so long ago. But as soon as I saw that field, all those memories came rushing back. Those long hours that we spent playing cricket under the afternoon sun, that walk back with a cricket bat in one hand and tossing the ball with the other.

But I guess things have changed now. I had not spoken to this guy for over eight years. I had stopped playing cricket and didn't have the balls to run around in the afternoon sun. In fact, a couple of paces of brisk steps and I would be left gasping for air. I looked around to see what else had changed. There used to be a small 'paan shop' at the corner where the road turned, and Bikash's home was right behind that shop. It was one landmark that I remembered distinctly. We used to spend a major portion of our pocket money here. Though it had been over 8 years, I was still expecting the same shaggy wooden shop at the corner.

"Raasta yaad to hai na?" GKD asked.

"Ha bhai, pura yaad hai. Lots of memories here."

"Saamne kone pe ek 'paan ka dukaan' tha wo waha," I added, pointing my finger at a distance, indicating roughly where this paan shop would be.

GKD followed me silently towards the pan shop. On reaching there, GKD mockingly said:

"Mast dukaan hai re..."

"Abe yahi to tha, must have shifted," I replied.

"But there... there is his room," I added after browsing through the neighborhood.

"Chal..." GKD said, leading the way. I stood there watching GKD, waiting for him to realize what he was doing wrong. After taking a few paces, GKD stopped, looked back, and said:

"Saale silently maar raha hai na. Chal aaja tu hi aagey aa." I smiled and walked towards the room.

We were so consumed with the thought of entering Gangtok that we did not wait to see the damage that the earthquake had caused in this region. On reaching his doorstep, I saw what this monstrous quake had done. There were visible cracks on the walls besides the door, describing them as cracks would be a major understatement; the walls, which once stood as a single entity, were split into two distinct sections. I could only imagine the damage it might have caused at places closer to the epicenter. I drew GKD's attention towards the fissure that was created by the movement of the plates underneath.

"Abe dekh be... Sasuri poora phaad hi diya hai."

"Haa be... pel diya hai pura."

I knocked at the door cautiously as if it would've collapsed if I knocked hard enough. A lady emerged from inside and said:

"Kas lai bhetnu chha," she asked whom I wanted to meet in broken Nepali. It seemed that her words had been soaked in a thick gravy of pain. Her eyes were filled with an indescribable anguish, and the most striking thing was that she was not trying to hide it. The pain in her words made its way into my heart. I was unable to reply and stood there staring at her long enough to make her uncomfortable. Seeing that I was making her uncomfortable, GKD elbowed me.

"Bikash hai kya aunty," even though general courtesy dictates that the reply should be made in the same language in which the question was asked, I, however, was unable to keep up with it. Nonetheless, I was expecting a reply, but all I got was a long, hard, blank gaze at my face by her. It seemed that she had somehow recognized me but was having difficulty placing me. I decided to help her out:

"Aunty mai uska friend... Gangtok me saath tha 'Kyi-De-Khang' school me... Ajit," I answered in syllables, expecting that it would be easier for her to process.

I was trying to explain my presence to her when a voice came from inside: "Kaun hai maa?" I cannot explain how thrilled I was on hearing that voice; I recognized it. It was Bikash.

"Ajit..." she replied in a confused tone. She was still unable to place me.

"Kya... Ajit..." he replied, limping his way out towards the door. My happiness reached a completely new level when I saw him; he had hardly changed in all these years; I had thought that I might not be able to recognize him, but it seemed that time had forgotten to have its effect on him.

"Arre yaar... Kaisa hai, dherai din bhayo." He asked how I was and also said that it had been a long time that we last met.

"Haa yaar, kaafi din ho gaye... Ab kya reason du..." I was at fault here; it usually takes two people to severe any relationship. This, however, was a case where I had severed it single-handedly. Bikash, on his part, had tried a lot to contact me; I was the one who did not have "time" to talk. Bikash looked at GKD, who was standing a couple of feet away, kicking away the small pebbles. I realized that I had not introduced the two of them yet.

"Oh... Sorry, GKD... This is Bikash, my school friend, and this is GKD, matlab... Gautam Kumar Das, hum college me isko yahi bulate the." They shook hands and exchanged a courteous smile.

"Come let's sit inside," Bikash asked. We went into the room; there were rubbles still there, we dodged those debris and went in. We followed Bikash inside his room; he showed us the bed to sit.

"Take off the shoes and make yourselves comfortable."

I kicked off my shoes and sat on the bed; GKD, for some reason, wasn't looking very comfortable taking off his shoes; he sat there resting his feet on the floor, and obviously, he kept his shoes on. I was there to ask for his help, and I didn't have a lot of time, but for some reason, I was unable to start the conversation, and GKD did not know Bikash well enough to start talking and ask for the favor. What I could not understand was why Bikash kept quiet; he generally was not the one whom you would see groping for words to start a conversation. After a couple of minutes of awkward silence, Bikash spoke out:

"So Ajit, what brings you here after all these years?" He spoke with tear-filled eyes. I could not understand why. I wanted to think that he was overwhelmed seeing me, but I knew this wasn't it; there was something that was bothering him.

"Abe why are you crying? ro kyu raha hai be..." I patted his back and asked as softly as possible. He quickly wiped his eyes with his palm.

"Kuchh nahi hai yaar... Bas yuhi. Ab batao, what made you remember me?" He asked.

"Yaar ek help chahiye tha... some advice actually," I thought there was no reason beating around the bush so I came straight to the point.

"Bol yaar... Will be more than happy to help," he said.

"Yaar, you know about the earthquake..."

"...Yes," I had not even completed my sentence when he cut me short.

It seemed that he didn't want the quake to be mentioned. However, I continued:

"Actually, there is a person there whom I need to contact. I am not able to get through the network, and I am worried about her well-being."

"Her..." He said, literally staring at me; he looked as if he was possessed. I wasn't sure why everything around seemed so weird of late, but again I had better things to worry about at this point, so there was no real reason for me to try and start reading in between lines here.

"Yes... Poorvi, you remember her, right?" I added.

"Arre sahi hai bhai, so you two are together now?"

"This man here was madly in love with her; in school, he always used to talk about her. I think we were in class 3 or 4 when he started," He added, turning towards GKD.

GKD just smiled back politely; he knew this story. However, it would not have been good if he said that he was aware of my story.

"Haa yaar, there is a whole lot of things that transpired between us. I'll tell you the entire story in detail later. Abhi bas itna samajh le ki I am dying inside because I don't know anything about her well-being". If I sat down to tell him the entire story, it would consume the whole day, and I did not have that kind of time at hand.

"So you want me to find out if she is ok?" Bikash asked.

"Actually, mai aur GKD Gangtok jaa rahe hain to find her. The problem is that we think we won't be allowed to enter the quake-hit region. So if you can help us arrange a vehicle, that'll be great," I told him what exactly I expected from him.

"See Ajit, I know that you no longer consider me your friend, but to show it right on my face, that's rude." I was surprised as to why he became so angry suddenly.

True, I had severed all contacts with him, and now I was here asking for a favor, but I knew he was pissed off at something else. If it had been me asking for a favor, he would have snapped when I mentioned that I needed a favor, not now when I explained what favor I needed.

"Aisa mat bol yaar... What did I do?" I asked for his clarification. He turned towards GKD and said:

"No offense, friend." Almost immediately, he turned his gaze towards me and said:

"You've known him for how long, maybe 4-5 years, right?" He said, pointing towards GKD. I understood where he was going with this, but I did not stop him; in order to vent off the anger/frustration within him, it was important that he spoke.

"...and we were friends since our diaper days, right?" He continued.

"...and you didn't even stop to at least consider including me in your journey." He was really emotional when it came to our friendship. I had to say something, something that would do some damage control.

"I understand your anger or frustration, whatever it is, it's not misplaced, but there is supposed to be a lot of danger where I am going. I don't want to be the reason behind my friends' suffering. To be honest, I didn't want to involve GKD in my endeavor, but he tricked me, and he's here. I don't want another friend of mine to embark on the path of death alongside me." I explained.

"Dude stop there... You've said enough; now let me talk," Bikash spoke.

"You want my help; you'll get it, but it won't come so easy."

"Name the price I'll have to pay, there is nothing I'll hesitate to do in exchange for your help and forgiveness," I said.

"I'm coming along with you," He replied even before I could complete my sentence. I could not reply; I was overwhelmed by his gesture. I looked towards GKD and then back to Bikash and thought how lucky I was. There are people who live their entire life without a friend, and here I was with two guys offering to come with me on my quest, a quest that was bound to present its share of difficulties. I knew there was no talking Bikash out of this; to be honest, I was kind of glad that he would be there with me. GKD was completely unfamiliar with the landscape there, and even though I had spent my entire life prior to college there, I was also quite thin as far as the knowledge of the terrain was considered. Also, I was kind of losing the fluency I once had over Nepali.

"Bikash, you, of all people, know the danger we are about to embark," I cautioned.

"Dude, you're talking as if we're going to a battlefield. True, there are aftershocks being felt, but it's not as dangerous as you are making it sound."

"Theek hai, maanta hu ki it's not as dangerous, but still it's not as safe as this house. You'll be walking into something that is completely damaged, there are no roads anymore, most of the bridges are gone, plus there are continuous landslides at the Singtam stretch." I tried to paint the picture of the quake-stricken region.

"To kya hua... It is a small price to pay considering what you want to achieve," GKD retaliated.

I once again did not understand what he really meant. Did he mean that me putting my friend's life in danger is a small price to pay for the end result? Now that he put this fact on my face, I started to think, was I really doing this, was I being so selfish?

"Yaar, there is nothing that is worth spending friends on," I replied. Thinking about the price that I might have to pay to meet Poorvi made me misty in the eyes; I wasn't ready to pay this price.

"Abe gadhe... Kya bakwaas kar raha hai, you haven't forced either of us to come with you. On the contrary, you always opposed this. If we let you go alone on this trip, that would be selfish on our part; there is no way that we would ever be able to explain our actions if we back out now." GKD said, and Bikash nodded hysterically.

"Yaar, tum log bhi chutiye ho... Saalau maroge to mujhe mat bolna," I said with a smile. I did not want to lose time and wanted to start the journey as soon as possible.

"Ajit... You probably don't understand the luck that you are in today," Bikash said. I looked towards GKD; he had said that if I was lucky, I would be able to meet Bikash, and now that I had met him, I did feel lucky.

"Bata yaar... I felt that I was lucky to meet you," I asked Bikash.

"Mera mama, Shyam mama, you remember right? He is in the army, and as luck would have it, today he is traveling to Gangtok with the relief distribution team. I think I can have him tag us along." Bikash said.

I was excited; actually, to say that I was excited would be an understatement. I was over the moon. I looked towards GKD and said:

"Yaar, this solves all our problems. The time we spent on the plane raking our brains coming up with ways to enter Gangtok has been put to waste by this one solution."

"Thanks a lot, Bikash, you do not understand the degree to which you have eased us." I was so happy that I was actually fumbling to find proper words.

"Arre bhai... Koi baat nahi re, you do not know what favor you've done by allowing me to come with you," Bikash said.

I didn't read in between lines here; all I thought was that he was happy to help a friend.

"Achchha, ye bataoo when will we start our journey... and yes, do you think aunty will allow you to go? She looks pretty shaken up." Amidst all the euphoria, I had completely forgotten that he was not staying alone. Unlike me and GKD, he could not keep this from his family.

"Ya... It will be a bit difficult to convince her, but I'll get her on board. Mamaji said that he'll be leaving at around 5 in the evening; you guys wait here; I'll talk to my mother and mamaji and be back. It's already past 3; we'll have to leave pretty soon," He said and left the room.

"Sahi hai yaar... Mast banda hai. You should be thankful that he met us, else can you imagine the problem that we would have had to face," GKD exclaimed.

"Haa yaar, but I still feel a bit guilty considering that he will be leaving his mother here all alone, especially when there are aftershocks been felt so frequently."

"Abe, ye to hai, but again ek raat ki hi to baat hai. Once we reach Gangtok, he can come back," GKD tried to pacify me, but he himself must have realized how feeble his argument was. I still pointed it out to him:

"Yaar, tujhe kya lagta hai wo hume Gangtok pahucha ke wapas aa jaega? I know him; he won't leave our side till we manage to find Poorvi. He'll do whatever it takes to find her."

"Still... It won't take much time, and by what I make of him, I don't think you'll be able to stop him. So just be grateful that you have him by your side."

"Nahi yaar, I am grateful that both of you are by my side. I couldn't thank you enough." I expressed my gratitude.

"Patti hero mat ban, saale agar ek baar bhi thanks bola to dekhna kya karta hu mai tera." I had practically invited this outburst; I knew how we guys from PZ reacted to thanks, I would have reacted the same way.

"Abe theek hai re... Nahi bolunga, khush? Magar tujhe lagta hai Bikash ki maa maan jaegi?" I asked.

"Haa maan jaegi aunty, Bikash samjha lega," GKD said. Now that Bikash had already taken care of our biggest problem, there was hardly anything for us to talk about. I mean it wasn't as if we did not have anything in common to talk about, but the situation was such.

"Aur bata tu kaisa hai, kaisi chal rahi hai zindagi?" I asked; we had not had a chance to ask about each other's well-being. Right from the moment we met, all we had done was plan, and now with Mamaji in the picture, things seemed to have fallen into place.

"Abe sab sahi hai, kaam theek thaak hai, magar you know it is no college. I can bear everything in Kolkata, but there is one thing that really gets on my nerves: it's the noise there. The city is never quiet; at times, it gets so loud that you can literally shoot a bullet, and no one would notice," He replied. The moment GKD mentioned Kolkata, my heart started racing. It was in Kolkata that we actually bonded and was one of the most important phases of my life with Poorvi.

"Abe sasuri Kolkata..." I exclaimed.

"Kya hua..." GKD did not know what importance Kolkata had in Poorvi's and my life.

"Abe Kolkata ke saath bahut saari memories attached hai," I said.

"Ohh... ok ok, koi baat nahi, chhod jaa hi rahe hain waha. Achchha ye bata mere diljale aashiq Poorvi ko call lag raha hai?" GKD asked.

"Abe nahi be, baal tension ho raha hai re pata nahi call kyu nahi lag raha," I expressed my concern.

"Ghabra mat be, saale major earthquake aaya tha, pure region me blackout hai; that is the reason why you are not able to reach her. But you don't worry, everything is going to be fine." GKD tried to soothe my aching soul, but even he knew that these words were not enough to console me. However, I appreciated the gesture.

"Haa be, thanks..." I replied.

We talked for a little while about how this trip would end up being a milestone in my love life. After some 20 minutes or so, Bikash re-entered the room and said:

"Guys, nikalte hai."

"So aunty is on board?" GKD asked.

"Yes, it was a bit difficult, but she understood," Bikash replied and led us outside the room.

There on the road stood a tall mustached man; he had an uncanny resemblance to the one I saw in my dream on the plane. I felt goosebumps because I distinctly remembered what he had said then, 'Chal pahucha deta hu tujhe jaha jaana hai,' and here he was taking me where I wanted to go. It could be a coincidence, but could it mean something else? Was there something supernatural going around here? I didn't believe in these kinds of things, but this made me rethink my beliefs.

"Uncle ye Ajit hai, bachpan me dekha tha aapne, yaad hai, aur ye iska dost Gautam," Bikash introduced us to Shyam mama.

"Nahi yaar, bahut din pehle ki baat hogi, ab to bada ho gaya hai ye kaafi," Shyam mama replied.

"Magar chalne se pehle ek baat yaad rakhna, the terrain is really hostile, be alert at all times." He added.

"Theek theek mama ji..." I replied for both me and GKD.

"Theek hai to phir chalo," He said, pointing towards the army van.

Chapter 10

ROAD-TRIP

We entered the van, Bikash sat beside Mamaji, who was driving it, and GKD and I sat at the back.

"Ajit, Gautam, koi dikkat to nahi hai na? Be careful and watch out for the falling boulders on the way," Mamaji cautioned us.

"Theek hai, Mamaji. We'll be careful," replied GKD.

I was still dwelling on the uncanny resemblance between Mamaji and the man on the plane. I was trying to reason with myself and come up with an explanation for this. I thought there was only one obvious explanation: I had dreamed about an army man on the plane, and seeing Mamaji in uniform must have recreated the image from the dream in my mind. This settled the uncanny resemblance, and apart from this, whatever questions I had in mind could safely, and to some extent correctly, be attributed to coincidence.

"Yaar Ajit, finally, it seems that things are falling into place. Dekhna sab theek hoga. Have you thought about what you're going to say to her after you meet? Baal kela... just imagine how romantic it'll be. A guy who has been separated from a girl for over 2 years finds out that an earthquake has hit the place where she was staying. He puts everything in line, his life, his job, to go and meet her. Saale, wo picture imagine kar raha hu jab tu uske paas aayega. I bet the expression on her face will be worth millions," GKD was picturing the climax of this journey even though we had just started it.

Nobody knew the danger we could walk into, but I guess it was GKD's method to keep the positive energy going. I just smiled at him. I obviously did not have anything prepared; how could I have done it? All this while, I was worried about getting there, and now that I was on this van with an army personnel, I should have been ecstatic, or at least I should've started thinking or planning about the things that I should say once I meet her. But there was something that was pegging me back. For some reason, I wasn't able to feel the ecstasy that I was supposed to feel.

"Abe kuchh plan nahi kiya hai. I think it would be a little premature to start thinking on these grounds now," I replied.

"Abe tu itna negative kab se ho gaya? Be positive; everything will be okay," GKD was just trying to lift me up.

"Mai negative nahi ho raha hu; I just don't want to count the chickens before they actually hatch," I tried to explain why I was not entertaining the thought of preparing something before I met her.

"But what is the harm? I do not see any problem in that," GKD, for some reason, was relentless.

"Dekh yaar, you don't want me to explain it to you using my trademark style, do you?" I was notorious for drawing analogies, and, to be honest, people did not always like it.

"Actually, I do. Let's see what you've got that can explain your thinking," GKD asked.

"Tell me what happens to your teeth when you drink something very cold after having something hot," I asked.

"The teeth hurt like hell," he replied.

"Exactly... I don't want to be that teeth," I asserted my logic.

"Chal theek hai, it's your call after all," GKD gave in to my logic.

"But the good news is that the analyzing, analogy-giving Ajit is back, and believe me, we need him," GKD added.

He was right. I had not realized that I was now able to think more clearly. Probably with time, the shock had settled down.

"Guys, be careful; we are entering the landslide zone," Bikash shouted at us.

I looked outside from the window and was amazed by what I saw. I called out loud to GKD, "Yaar, bahar dekh, kya mast scene hai re..."

"Pagal ho gaya hai kya? How can you see the beauty amidst all this destruction?" GKD was not amused by my observation.

To be honest, even I was not very thrilled by my vision. I mean, how could I see the beauty in something that is at best the result of a major natural calamity. "Abe, I can't help but observe it," I replied.

"And what do you observe that 'turns' you on?" GKD's gesture of using air quotes was a bit hurtful but not completely misplaced.

"Abe bahar dekh, these hills that you see were completely covered in green. All these years, the only color known to these hills was green. And just see now, the mudslide has left a harrowed impression on it; it has changed. These new muddish yellow colors, dotted with the already present green. The dents that have been created by the uprooted trees and the falling boulders are painting quite a picture. Yaar, just try to forget about the damage and the destruction. If you see it as an individual, independent image, you'll probably enjoy it," I said, trying to paint a picture describing what I actually saw there.

Looking at his expression, he did not seem very excited. "Believe me, Ajit, you perplex me. Matlab abhi kuchh der pehle you were saying that you are upset and won't be able to think clearly until you see Poorvi, and now you are seeing the 'inherent' beauty because you are able to see it as an individual, independent image. I just don't understand how can you?" GKD was surprised, to say the least, at my 'individual and independent' remark.

We were busy arguing over the apparent beauty of the valley when Bikash shrieked, "Abbbeeee!" And with that sound, we heard a loud thud. Something hit the vehicle, and the next thing I saw was Shyam Mamaji desperately trying to steer the vehicle through the uneven rubbled remains of the road. The road, which was more an extension of the hill. The wet mud, along with the decaying leaves and other organic matter, made it literally impossible for the tires to find a grip of any sort. We continued to slide. I was squished against the window, and GKD was pushing against me. Everything happened so fast that there was barely any time to react or even think about what should be done. The van hit something, and it stopped almost suddenly, throwing us out of our seats towards the driver's seat.

I banged my head hard against something. I felt my head; I was bleeding. Blood started flowing from the open wound, dripping through the side of my head, along my ears, onto the floor of the destroyed van. I slowly picked myself up, looked around to see the well-being of others around. GKD lay just beside me, his hands were jammed underneath the front seat that had collapsed. I lifted my head to see where Bikash and Shyam Mamaji were; they were not inside the vehicle. They must have been thrown out, I thought. I inched towards GKD. Apart from the jammed hand, he was fine. There were no other signs of physical injury. I had seen in movies that after an accident, vehicles usually blow up. It's not that I thought the vehicle would blow off, still, I wanted to get the hell out of there as soon as I could.

“Abe GKD... Theek hai na?” I called out.

“Haa be... tu?” He replied in a weak, feeble voice.

“Haa, theek hu, ruk, tera haath nikalta hu.” I said and started to look for openings through which I could glide his hands out. There was nothing there; his hand was completely jammed under the front seat. It seemed as if the floor of the van was embracing the seat, and GKD's hand was trying to stop it. I started to lift the seat. The blood draining out of my head was making me weak. I summoned all my energy and tried to lift the wrecked seat. Due to the effort that I put in, pressure on my head increased, and the blood started gushing out from my wound. I was rapidly losing strength because of the incessant blood loss. I had to do something to stop the flow and do it fast. I tore up a rag long enough from my shirt to tightly secure the wound. I looked at GKD; he was not moving. I had to pull him out before he passed out; if he did pass out, pulling him out would be a herculean task. I patted his head and asked:

"Oye GKD, theek hai tu? Sun raha hai mujhe?" He shook his head in affirmative.

"Listen, I'll push the seat up, and I want you to try and free your hand. When I say 'NOW,' please put all your strength into pulling your arm out," I shouted at the top of my voice. This was a perilous situation, with boulders rolling down the hill. I desperately wanted to free us before one of those boulders struck the van.

"Okay," GKD replied.

Summoning every ounce of my energy, I managed to lift the seat slightly. Just then, I yelled, "NOW!" However, I couldn't maintain the effort long enough for GKD to pull his arm out.

"Sorry, yaar," I said, panting. "No worries, we'll try again. Summon all your energy, GKD. If you don't pull your hand out, we'll be stuck here. Do you understand? We can't stay here for long. Let me try lifting the seat again, and you pull your arm out when I say."

I attempted to motivate him, though I was struggling myself. I couldn't show any signs of weakness.

"Get ready," I instructed GKD.

I summoned all my energy, the seat lifted a bit, just then I yelled “NOW”. But I was not able to hold for long enough for GKD to pull his arm out.

“Sorry yaar... Chal mai phir uthata hu, pull your arm out when I say” I tried to pep him up, I myself was not feeling strong but I could not let myself become weak here I called upon all my strength and tried to lift the seat. “Nikaal” I shouted...

“Yeeeaaaahhhh... Aaaahhhh.... Maaaakaaaaa... Nikal gaya.” GKD yelled out, he was seething in pain still he managed to pull his hands out.

I sat down clinching my head, the blood had soaked my already torn shirt, there was hardly any inch there that was not dripping of my own blood. I looked at GKD, his arm was fully peeled, there was no skin cover left on his right arm, blood was oozing out and he was howling in pain.

“Koi baat nahi... chal bahar chal, bahar dekhte hai” I tried to pacify GKD, frankly speaking I was in no condition to speak, I could see spots around me, I was sure that I would collapse if I tried to stand up but I could not show a moment of physical weakness.

I felt responsible for his condition. If I had convinced him not to come with me, he might have been safe. I kicked open the door and dragged my weakened, blood-soaked body out of the wreckage. GKD followed, his arm a horrifying sight with no skin covering it, blood gushing out like a fountain. Both of us crawled toward the roadside, lying there restlessly. We pressed cloth against our wounds to staunch the bleeding. I was barely aware of our surroundings; I couldn't even recall where we were. I knew we were injured, I had lost a lot of blood, and GKD was in terrible pain, but that was the extent of my awareness. I may even say that I was unconscious—not entirely, but far from conscious. After some time, the bleeding stopped, but the pain intensified as the adrenaline wore off. I held my head in my hands and looked at GKD, who lay on the ground with his mouth open and drooling. His injured arm rested against his chest, and the blood was beginning to clot. I felt profound sadness for his condition and blamed myself for what had happened. I had to accept that I was just as helpless as he was.

"Hey, GKD, are you still with me?" I asked, attempting a forced laugh.

"Yeah, I'm here," he replied weakly.

The way he spoke sent a shiver down my spine. He was genuinely weak, and words were reluctant to leave his mouth. After a while, when I had regained some strength, I decided to search for Shyam mamaji and Bikash.

"GKD, stay here. I'm going to look for Bikash and Shyam mamaji. Will you be okay?" I asked.

He nodded in response, which emphasized his weakness. If he had been capable, he would never have let me go alone. I worried about leaving him behind, but Bikash was also in this situation because of me, and I couldn't leave him. I stood up, still pressing the rag against my head, which was saturated with blood. My legs were shaky, but I pressed on. Ideally, I should have shouted for Bikash and mamaji, but I could barely muster the strength to stand, let alone shout. I hoped they were somewhere nearby. I stumbled through the rubble, struggling to stay on my feet. The dead leaves and mud from the hill made the ground incredibly slippery, and I kept bumping into boulders, uprooted trees, and broken trunks. I didn't even stop to see what I was colliding with; I focused all my energy on moving forward. I collided with an obstruction, fell flat on what I thought was the ground, and realized that this was the last thing I needed. I was barely capable of standing, let alone lifting myself up. I was already on the brink, and this fall pushed me over the edge. I felt like I was about to lose consciousness. I imagined the scene that had unfolded as a result of my recklessness. I was lying there, almost unconscious, with GKD probably writhing in agony from his severely injured arm. Bikash and mamaji were missing, and the army van was crushed to the ground. This was not the right time for such thoughts, but for some reason, I managed to smile. I wanted to laugh at my predicament, but all I could muster was a feeble smile. I wondered if I had really wanted to reunite with Poorvi at the cost of my friend's life. The damage had been done, and I could only hope there were no casualties and that everyone was okay. I was unable to stay awake any longer; I was rapidly losing consciousness. Then, I heard a squeaky voice from below.

"Hey!" someone shouted. This was followed by a deep sigh. I rolled down from my perch, thinking I had fallen to the ground, and looked in the direction of the voice. I was thrilled by what I saw—thrilled would be an understatement. There were no words to describe the ecstasy I felt: it was Bikash.

"Are you okay?" I asked, though weak, I managed to utter the words.

"Yeah, I'm fine," Bikash replied, not sounding too weak.

I was relieved to see that he seemed to be in good shape. I opened one eye to see what was happening, and another pleasant surprise awaited me: Bikash stood up and dusted himself off. I silently thanked God for showing mercy and closed my eye again.

"Hey, Ajit, are you okay? Where are the others?" Bikash asked, trying to help me up. This was it; I finally received the help my body had been desperately craving. When a wounded and weary body receives support of any kind, it tends to relax, allowing wounds to be tended to. That's exactly what happened—I blacked out.

"Ajeettt... Ajeeetttttt... Where's Gautam?" someone shook me vigorously and kept asking about GKD. I felt water being splashed on my face and then forced down my throat.

I came back to life. I opened my eyes and saw Shyam mamaji, who didn't appear very injured, but I suspected he was skilled at masking any injuries, being an army man.

"Where's Gautam?" Shyam mamaji asked directly. I drank the water, but I still didn't have enough energy to walk or speak. So, I just pointed toward the spot where I had left GKD. It shouldn't have been too far, and I hoped mamaji would find him. In the meantime, Bikash stayed with me, continuously offering me water. After some time, I had enough strength to talk, and I asked him about his condition.

"Did you get hurt badly?" I inquired.

"Come on, we're fine. Just relax," Bikash replied.

"But... how did you manage to escape?" I asked softly.

"When the boulder hit, the front door opened. We held on to our seats as long as we could, but then the van struck a tree, and we lost our grip and were thrown out. Fortunately, we didn't collide with any hard surfaces," Bikash explained.

"But you were unconscious, right?" I asked again.

"I can't explain it; perhaps it was the spinning, perhaps being thrown out of the car, or who knows what, but I'm perfectly fine. So, what happened to you and Gautam?" Bikash asked.

"After the van was hit by the boulder, we were thrown toward the front seat. Something hit my head, and GKD's arm was jammed under the front seat. I managed to free both of us, left him on the side of the road, and came out searching for you two," I explained.

I lay there on the ground with my eyes closed, trying to piece together the ordeal we had just endured. It was nothing short of terrifying, but the silver lining was that, apart from me, no one had suffered serious injuries. I considered my injury serious due to the head wound, and the extent of damage was uncertain. Moreover, I had lost what felt like a gallon of blood.

Chapter 11

FINAL LAP

"They are here," Bikash said. I was relieved to hear that they had arrived. I wasn't in good shape, and I wasn't sure how much longer I could hold myself together. Knowing that GKD was fine was a huge relief for me. I had lost a significant amount of blood, and as a result, I was incredibly weak. I was so weak that I couldn't even open my eyes properly. I mustered all the remaining energy I had and managed to open one eye. From the corner of that eye, I saw GKD and Mamaji approaching. Mamaji appeared composed and determined, which made me wonder how he was able to remain so composed after everything that had happened. He must have seen and experienced worse, and perhaps in situations like these, the best emotion to have was no emotion at all.

"Ajit, are you okay?" Mamaji asked, his voice barely audible.

"Ajit, are you with me?" he continued, shaking me gently.

"Yes, Mamaji, I'm fine, it's just that my head is spinning a bit," I replied. I could hear my voice, and I sounded weak, extremely weak. But I felt that I couldn't afford to show any physical weakness at this moment.

"Okay, let's see if you can stand up," Mamaji ordered. I felt a surge of irritation. I was struggling to even speak, let alone stand, and here he was asking me to get up. However, what I failed to realize was that I wasn't defying the orders of a civilian; it was an army man who was giving the orders, and he wouldn't just stand by and let me have my way. He repeated his command, this time with an authoritative tone.

"Stand up," he said sternly. "You're saying that you're fine, just a bit of dizziness, right? So what's stopping you? Get on your feet, you little prick..."

I had no choice but to respond to his demands. Summoning every ounce of my remaining energy, I managed to stand up. I looked into his eyes, staring intently, as if trying to make a statement. Then, unexpectedly, I began to vomit, as if all the bravado I had wrapped up in that stare had evaporated, and I was now spewing like an open hydrant.

"You have a concussion, Ajit. You need medical attention," Mamaji said. I realized that he had been so aggressive earlier to assess the extent of my injury, which was quite severe.

"But, Mamaji, I don't want to slow us down. We have to reach Gangtok first," I said.

"Yes, we do have to reach, and reach alive," he replied. "There's an army camp about 3 kilometers from here. We'll have to stop there and patch you up first."

"Can you guys walk that far?" he asked.

I contemplated my response. My heart was telling me that I could walk that distance, that I should walk, that I couldn't be the one holding our team back. But my body was clearly not cooperating.

"Yes, Mamaji, I can walk," I replied after a moment's thought. I knew it was going to be a challenging endeavor, but I was determined.

"Okay, guys, let's start," Mamaji signaled. We began to follow him, with GKD and Bikash on either side of me, although neither of them physically held me. I didn't like anyone helping me in that way, at least as long as I could stand and walk on my own. My mind was still focused on my ultimate goal: reaching Gangtok and ensuring Poorvi's safety. That was my primary agenda.

As we walked, I began to think about the accident and the earthquake's aftermath. It was a terrifying experience, and I couldn't help but wonder what had happened to those who had experienced the full force of the earthquake. I had been confident that Poorvi was safe, but now I started to doubt that assumption. What if she wasn't so lucky? My thoughts raced, and I felt a growing restlessness. It was as if Poorvi was reaching out to me, and I had to catch hold of her before she slipped away again.

"Ajit, don't run. You'll tire yourself out," GKD shouted as I picked up the pace.

But I couldn't slow down. I felt an urgent need to reach Poorvi as quickly as possible, as if she were in trouble and needed me. I ran with my eyes fixed on the ground, occasionally lifting my head to ensure I was on the right path. I was running blindly, driven by an overwhelming desire to reunite with her.

"Ajit, stop!" GKD cried out.

But there was no way I was going to slow down. It felt as though Poorvi was within reach, and I couldn't let her escape again. I ran with all my remaining strength, my determination pushing me forward.

"Ajit, stop!" GKD yelled once more.

Suddenly, I felt someone lifting me from behind. I tried to resist, but I couldn't. I looked down to see that it was Mamaji who had picked me up. He had lifted me onto his shoulders as if I were a wounded soldier in a battlefield. It was a strange sight, but it increased our speed. I was the weakest member of the team at that moment, and my body was on the verge of giving out.

"Ajit, tell me about this Poorvi girl you're going to meet," Mamaji asked.

I was getting annoyed. Was this really the time for such questions? Mamaji was carrying an injured person on his shoulder, and I thought his top priority would be to reach safety as quickly as possible.

"She studies in Manipal," I replied, my voice slurring.

"Okay, so how did you two meet?" Mamaji continued with his questions.

I was growing frustrated with the conversation, but before I could respond, I started dozing off. Mamaji shook me awake.

"Ajit, don't you dare fall asleep now," he warned. "We're almost there. Just stay with me."

I understood that he didn't want me to fall asleep due to the concussion. I had done my best to stay awake, but now I could finally let go.

"We're here," someone said, and I was relieved to hear those words. I was in a place where I could receive medical attention, and the sooner I was treated, the sooner I could see Poorvi again.

"Can I get a chair here?" Mamaji called out. After a while, a man arrived with a wheelchair, and Mamaji carefully placed me in it. They wheeled me inside, where a doctor was expected. I was struggling to keep my head up, but after all the effort I had put into staying awake, I could now let myself relax.

"Onto the bed, slowly and carefully. He has head injuries, possibly even a concussion," Mamaji explained to the person helping me. They placed me on the bed, with all three of them gathered around me. I appreciated their concern, but I was also aware that there were other injuries to be addressed. GKD's hand must have been causing him immense pain, and I didn't want him to be here with me while he was in pain.

"Mamaji, how is Gautam's injury? Doesn't he need medical attention?" I asked.

"It's mostly external, nothing to worry about. I'll have his wound cleaned and bandaged. Bikash, stay with him. The doctor will be here shortly. In the meantime, don't let him fall asleep. We can't take any chances if it's a concussion," Mamaji instructed Bikash before walking away with GKD.

"Hey, Ajit, what an adventure, right?" Bikash said, trying to engage me in conversation. I looked at him and smiled. I knew why he was saying this—it wasn't because he genuinely believed this was an adventure; he was just trying to keep me engaged and not make any references that might strain me further. I smiled because I thought to myself, "Dude, you're smart, but I'm smarter."

After his statement, Bikash fell silent. I understood his dilemma. He couldn't talk about how horrifying the accident had been, he couldn't talk about Poorvi, and he probably didn't want to talk about himself. He didn't want to talk about Poorvi, but I did. She was the only person on my mind, and I was growing increasingly restless. I was on the verge of becoming paranoid, and even though I was trying my best to hold myself together, deep down, I knew that things could go terribly wrong.

All the destruction caused by the earthquake was visible, and it was far from pretty. I couldn't help but worry about Poorvi being trapped in one of those collapsed buildings. As my fear for her escalated, tears began to stream down my face.

"Ajit, kya hua? Why are you crying?" Bikash asked.

"Yaar... Poorvi theek to hogi na? Will she be fine? Will I get to see her ever again? Will I be able to explain to her how I feel?" My eyes were filled with tears, and they began to stream down my cheeks uncontrollably.

"Arre yaar... Why are you being so negative? You'll definitely meet her. Do you think everything that has happened to us today will go in vain? Does all of this suffering mean nothing? No, Ajit, I refuse to believe that after all we've been through, things would go wrong," Bikash reassured me. He had a passionate outburst of emotions, trying to lift my spirits.

I wanted to believe him, truly, but for some inexplicable reason, I couldn't. It felt as if something wasn't right. I had this nagging feeling that Poorvi might be in trouble, calling out to me, and I needed to respond. I was frustrated with my own body for holding me back. If it weren't for my physical limitations, I would have been closer to finding Poorvi and ensuring her well-being.

"Is the pain that excruciating?" asked the doctor, suddenly appearing in the room.

I hadn't even noticed him coming in, and his question caught me off guard. Tears were still streaming down my face, and it wasn't a sight the doctor was likely accustomed to, especially not in an army hospital.

"No, it's not that bad, still bearable," I replied, trying to regain my composure.

"So, what's with all those tears?" the doctor inquired.

I didn't want to delve into the emotional turmoil I was experiencing, so I remained silent. Fortunately, he seemed to understand my reticence and proceeded with his examination.

I was familiar with the routine doctors used to check for concussions. The doctor began with standard tests, such as checking my pupils' response to light. He took out a flashlight from his coat pocket and shone it into my eyes. It reminded me of a scene from the Bollywood movie "Munna Bhai MBBS" where the protagonist gets furious when a doctor flashes a light into his eyes. Though this situation was different, I couldn't help but draw a parallel.

"Okay, this looks fine," the doctor said. "Now, keep your eyes fixed on the tip of the flashlight." He held the light vertically and moved it closer to me, back and forth several times. Finally, he delivered his verdict, "This is also good."

I knew what would come next—those mundane, straightforward questions designed to assess cognitive function.

"What is your name?" the doctor began.

"Ajit."

"Which date is it today?"

"19th September 2011."

"Where are you right now?"

I paused for a moment. I wasn't sure if he meant my current physical location or my mental state. After a brief contemplation, I replied, "On the bed of an army hospital somewhere between Sevok and Singtam."

The doctor seemed to understand my response, and his smile indicated as much.

"Okay, you've answered what I needed to know, and more. I can say with a high degree of certainty that you don't have a severe concussion. The symptoms Shyam mentioned must be due to blood loss and weakness," he declared.

His assessment was encouraging, and I felt relieved. The last thing I wanted was to be deemed physically unfit to continue the journey.

"That's great news. I'm relieved," I said.

"Well, don't be," the doctor replied curtly.

His response caught me off guard. Not having a concussion should have been good news, but he seemed to be suggesting otherwise.

"You've lost a significant amount of blood, and I mean a significant amount. Because of this, your blood pressure has fallen to an alarmingly low level. What you need right now is complete rest and food," the doctor explained.

His words hit me like a ton of bricks. I started fearing the worst. It wasn't that he had said I was fatally weak; it was the implication that he might try to prevent me from continuing the journey. That was the last thing I wanted. I thought about the others who had come all this way, endured everything alongside me, and I worried that they might side with the doctor and try to stop me.

"But doctor, I can't stay. I have to be somewhere urgently. I can't stay here, please give me some injections or something. I can't stay back; I simply can't," I pleaded, arguing like a child. However, I knew my chances of convincing him were slim. He must have seen it all before.

"Ajit, what he's saying is for your own good. You can't even stand, let alone walk," Bikash interjected, advising me not to argue with the doctor.

I was distraught, but there was no way I was letting these guys stop me from going forward; every time Poorvi's image flashed before my eyes, my restlessness increased. This wasn't where I was supposed to be; I should have been with Poorvi.

"Bikash... what did the doctor say?" Mamaji asked.

"He is not having concussions but has lost a lot of blood because of which he is weak..." Bikash replied.

"GKD... haath kaisa hai re tera?" I asked.

"Abe baal kya batau be... these nurses here do not feel anything, they poured Dettol on my open wound man... And then when I expressed my pain, they laughed, they laughed because it was 'just an external injury.' Behenchod..."

I knew GKD had a low threshold for pain, and he was venting his frustration off.

"Mamaji, we should go from here, by the way, where exactly are we?" GKD asked.

"Just outside the campus of SMIT," Mamaji replied.

"But how come we did not see it?" GKD asked again.

"Because it is destroyed, and nobody pointed it out to you that you are passing by the debris of the SMIT," Mamaji replied.

"This is a temporary camp where the injured are patched up immediately and then transferred to other facilities based on the severity of the injury," Mamaji continued.

When I heard the name "SMIT," my heart almost skipped a beat; this was Poorvi's college; there were lots of memories associated with this place. But the funniest thing was that while I was thinking about the college and recollecting the past memories that I had there, it never occurred to me that he also said that the place was completely demolished. Suddenly I saw the doctors and the nurses run towards the exit; I was surprised to see this rush. Mamaji held one of the ward boys and asked him the reason for this commotion; he replied:

"Army managed to cut through a portion of the girls' hostel, 9 bodies have been discovered. We are not sure how many of them are alive."

This was the final nail in the coffin; I lost it completely, and there was no way that I was going to sit through this. I started struggling my way out of the bed; there was a host of needles and tubes that they had inserted in my body; I plucked those out.

"Pagal ho gaya hai kya? What the hell do you think you are doing? Marna hai kya. Just stay put here," Mamaji yelled out at me when he saw me plucking those needles out.

"I am going there, and I don't care if my body is strong enough to bear this. We have come this far, faced these many difficulties, survived that horrific accident, all for one reason: I am not letting these doctors' words stop me from doing what I, rather we, had started out to accomplish," I replied in a way that made it clear that I was not going to cave in this time around and that I meant business here.

It was the worst fear that I was going through; I knew that Poorvi was in college that fateful day. I had come here, all this was to find out if she was fine, but actually we had never considered what if she wasn't fine. What if the last thing that she ever said to me was "I love you Ajit," and to that I had replied, "I am not completely over you." Were those going to be the last words that we ever exchanged? How could I live with this realization for the rest of my life? No, this can't be the way it ends; she has to be alive; she must have survived. As these thoughts entered my mind, my eyes filled up, my throat started choking up; this was the emotional turmoil I was expecting not to face.

We started walking; the enthusiasm somehow had managed to get me out of the bed. But after a while, I realized this body had a mind of its own; howsoever hard I tried to convince myself that weakness was not an option, my body just wouldn't listen. It kept saying back, 'Dude, accept it, I am weak.' Watching my staggering steps and tears flowing out, GKD came up and said:

"Never give up until it's really over."

Mamaji overheard GKD, and he was no stranger to what I had been going through; he came up to me and patted my shoulders and said:

"There is a famous war story; once in a war, a platoon was surrounded by enemies. One by one, everyone was killed, barring the commander and a soldier. The commander said, 'I think we should surrender; we've lost the battle.' To this, the soldier replied, 'How come? I still have 1 bullet left.' Do you see what I want to tell? Never accept defeat until you are defeated."

Mamaji wasn't a person of many words, but what he said and what GKD said surely made sense but only to sane minds. I was insane, paranoid at that moment; I was not in a position to extract meaning from sentences at that moment.

I just nodded and started walking towards the rubble; with every step, my anxiety increased. I started praying harder, praying for her safety; it was as if I knew she was one among those nine. The place was cordoned off, and one by one the army guys were bringing in the casualties; GKD and Bikash stood by my side while Mamaji went to help those guys. And then suddenly I saw it, the spectacle that I had dreaded the most: on a stretcher carried by two people, there was a girl, head smashed, left side completely battered being taken away.

'Pakad lena... Please... Der mat karna,' all this while I was thinking that these were just random words that I had in that nightmare, but alas, it was more than just "random."

Today my Poorvi is being taken away on this stretcher; if only I had managed to come earlier and find her. She must have been trapped in this rubble for over 24 hours; there was every chance that the love of my life would have been fighting the inevitable, hoping that someone might come and rescue her. Unfortunately, that help did not come; I was too slow to reach here, and now I would never get to see the end of it. The one person that I had loved more than life itself was no more, and the worst part was that it happened when she had professed her love for me, and I did not respond; the last memory that she had of me was me saying that I was not sure if I loved her anymore, and well, she gave me the punishment I deserved. She left me to live with this guilt.

All this while in my head, I was thinking of the things I would say to her when we meet; I had imagined the look on her face when I would go to her and say that I was in love with her and would like to spend my life with her. Least did I know that this was how things were going to end. My eyes grew hazy; I could feel a lump in my throat. As the person holding the stretcher took Poorvi past me, I tried to scream; I wanted them to stop; I wanted to have a final look at her, bid her goodbye; I wanted to go up to her and say that I loved her and was really sorry for everything that I had intentionally or unintentionally done to her. With my heart filled with regret and sorrow, I stepped forward towards her; my heart started racing, tears started flowing, and then everything around me started spinning; there were spots being formed in front of my eyes; I could not go any further; I collapsed, and everything went blank thereon.

"Ajit..." I couldn't believe that I was hearing these words. After I had collapsed at SMIT, Mamaji, GKD, and Bikash took me to the hospital; I was kept under observation for over 24 hours; I was been given blood externally. Also, I was not in a position to have solid food; so there was another needle inserted to enable me to have liquid food. All in all, I was a mess; doctors were surprised at the slow progress I was making; all I had was a shortage of blood, but my vitals were dropping at an alarming rate. Actually, after I thought that Poorvi was no more, I had given up all desire to live.

She was all I could think of, the sweet memories that we had together, but those memories were never lived long as all those memories ended with the picture that was engraved in my mind: Poorvi being carried away by the army people on the stretcher. So when I heard the word, I was shocked; for me, Poorvi was dead; I had seen her, and now I was hearing her voice. I was shocked, to say the least; I was hoping that this was not one of those nightmare episodes that I had on the plane. I was looking towards her with wide, unflinching eyes, almost in disbelief. She noticed my disbelief; it was written all over my face.

I was constantly gazing at her face, and in return, she was simply smiling. The smile was coming through from her lips, but somehow it didn't reach her eyes; the same eyes which at one point had twinkled were now blank. She was probably finding it difficult to believe that I had come all the way from Bangalore to meet her. She started coming towards me; she came close to my headrest and punching my arm she said:

"Aaye kyu..." As she said these words, her eyes filled up; she was crying, crying for me. This was the happiest moment in my life. The way she said those words marked her concerns for me; those concern was truly genuine. I don't know what was there in that punch; it was kind of magical; I forgot all my pain; my heart was overwhelmed; only a true romantic can come close to understanding what I was going through. I was so ecstatic that everything around me seemed to be going in slow motion; I was not at all bothered about what was around me; for me, the world was Poorvi, and she was standing right besides me.

My ecstasy was amplified all the more because of the fact that I had thought that I had seen the end of her; I had thought that the person I had seen on that stretcher was Poorvi and I would never be able to see her again; but not only was she alive, she was unharmed and standing right in front of me.

"Poorvi... I'm glad..." I couldn't finish my sentence; the fact that she was alive overwhelmed me to the brim. "Me too," she replied and stood there running her fingers over my hair.

Both of us were crying, but I'm sure none of us were grieving; these in real sense were tears of joy.

"Abe had hai yaar... kab se bahar ruka tha, expecting that koi to hume mention karega aur hum ek dramatic entry maarenge, magar tum log to bhool hi gaye hume." GKD walked in along with Bikash.

Actually, I had completely forgotten about them; I was so busy trying to soak in the fact that Poorvi was standing in front of me that I had forgotten that the world even existed. It was then that I realized that I had not asked the most obvious question; how she knew I was here?

"Arre sorry yaar... to be honest I just... you know..." I was not finding the correct set of words to explain myself.

"But how did she know I was here?" I asked. GKD and Bikash looked at each other, and then Bikash started saying:

"After you collapsed, we rushed you back to the camp; along with you, there were three other girls who had survived with minor scratches, nothing serious at all. I mean minus, of course, the trauma. It was then that I thought we ask them about Poorvi as you had not told us anything about her."

Bikash added the last sentence with a frown; I realized how stupid I had been to not tell them more about Poorvi.

Bikash continued: "We went up to a girl and started telling her about our journey; I mentioned Poorvi's name, expecting to get some information out of her, and just like it happens in movies, another girl overheard us and asked: 'Sorry... but are you talking about Ajit from Silchar?'"

"Remember my roommate Meenu, Meenu Verma... wahi thi," Poorvi filled me in.

"Yes... Meenu, she was aware of the little situation that was going on between you two, and luckily for us, she was right there and gave us her address; we took Mamaji's permission, drove all the way to Church road, found her, told her about our little adventure, and brought her here." If seeing Poorvi was not enough, this was, I was not sure what I was happier for... meeting Poorvi after I thought she was no more or at the gesture shown by my friends.

ACKNOWLEDGEMENT

I take this opportunity to thank all those who were involved in the making of this book directly or indirectly. Without your support this could not have been achieved. Looking forward to your support in my future projects as well.

Cheers!!!

www.ingramcontent.com/pod-product-compliance
Lightning Source LLC
LaVergne TN
LVHW041203150826
845673LV00001B/271

* 9 7 9 8 8 9 1 3 3 8 8 6 9 *